WOMEN
OF THE
PLAINS

WOMEN
OF THE
PLAINS

BRANDON S. PILCHER

Open Books Press
Saint Louis, Missouri

Published by Open Books Press, USA

www.OpenBooksPress.com
info@OpenBooksPress.com

An imprint of Pen & Publish, LLC
www.PenandPublish.com
Saint Louis, Missouri
(314) 827-6567

Print ISBN: 978-1-956897-32-6
eBook ISBN: 978-1-956897-33-3
Library of Congress Control Number: 2023945194

Printed on acid-free paper.

CHAPTER ONE
The Leopard and the Gazelle

Eastern Africa, 100,000 years ago

The sun broiled with cruel intensity high above the savanna. A herd of gazelle huddled on the bank of a shrunken waterhole beneath the shade of flat-topped acacia trees, drinking and dipping their faces into the water for relief from the scorching heat. Their sideways eyes kept watch for the slightest movements around them, while their twitching ears listened for the faintest noises. Predator or prey, every denizen of the plains had to be wary at every moment.

The eldest doe in the herd cocked her head to sniff the air. She thought she had spied the glint of dark eyes between yellowed blades of elephant grass behind her herd. Was it a hare or some other small animal looking at her? Or something more dangerous? A second and then a third scan revealed nothing more suspicious. With a confused grunt, the doe returned to drinking beside her mates.

Yet, she had not seen wrong.

Downwind of the herd, three women, each over twenty rainy seasons of age, crept in a triangular formation through the grass with flawless silence. Perspiration glossed their black-skinned figures, which were clad only in hide loincloths and tops. Slung over their backs under python-skin sashes were spears tipped with obsidian points. Flint knives rested on their hips.

Oja crawled ahead of the others in formation, advancing within striking distance of the nearest gazelle. She raised herself to a half-crouched position, the tips of the grass tickling above her waist, and slipped out her spear. As she drew her throwing arm back as far as she could, the weapon trembled in her grip. Her stomach growled deep inside like a famished lioness.

The dry season had gone on for over a month longer than normal. Oja had already seen her grandmother shrivel up and perish from both thirst and hunger earlier in the season, a sight that would scar her memory forever. The old woman had been their band's third loss this year. If the rains did not come before the next full moon, at least a third of the whole band might starve to death.

Oja could not let that happen. She and her hunting companions needed to bring home as much fresh meat as they could on this hunt. They had already spent the entire morning stalking it.

She looked to each of her friends, Uru to her left and Namak to her right, both still lying prone within the grass. They nodded to her, a signal that it was the right time to attack.

With one forward swing of her arm, Oja launched the spear at the gazelle she had been eyeing. The spear whistled through the air, glanced off her quarry's hip, and landed with a loud thud into the trunk of a nearby acacia. The wounded gazelle bleated as it and the rest of the herd sprang into a gallop, disappearing past the reeds and trees on the waterhole's far side.

Shaking her hand up at the sun, Oja growled a curse. "How could you make me miss, O ancestors?"

"Don't blame *them*," Namak said. "It's not their fault you can't aim."

Oja shot her friend a snarling glare. "Do you want me to make meat out of you?"

"Quiet, you two!" Uru interjected. "Let's not bicker like children when we could be tracking them."

She walked over to the tree Oja's spear had hit, plucked it out of the bark, and handed it back. Uru then pointed to a droplet of blood sliding down a blade of grass where the missile had hit the gazelle. Impressed into the dusty soil beneath it were hoofprints that pointed northward.

Hunching their torsos so they did not stick up above the vegetation, the three women glided across the savanna in the direction the gazelles had fled. They kept as close as they could to the trail of tracks and trampled grass, finding them sprinkled with drops of blood. Oja offered a silent prayer to her ancestors, apologizing for cursing them and hoping they would cause the herd to tire and slow before sundown.

The sun, having already reached its zenith in the heavens, embarked on a gradual downward journey to the summits of the hills in the distant west, the sky's color shifting from bright blue to orange. Although the heat had relaxed over the day's passing, Oja's calves still strained from the nonstop hiking. Her heart thumped like a drumbeat as she panted.

She stopped when she spotted tawny forms within the grass. Several yards in front of the trio, the gazelle gathered in a tight circle near a copse of marula trees. The one her spear had barely hit grazed in the center of the herd, showing a slight limp as it milled around. Oja took out her spear again. She made sure to aim higher than before so that it would fly over the other animals and into her quarry. She would not miss it a second time.

Before she could release her weapon, the herd bolted into flight again. This time, the gazelles did not run straight away from their positions, but veered to the left. Behind them, a mottled black-and-yellow blur pounced onto the already injured gazelle and brought it down, growling over the antelope's frail bleating until the latter surrendered with a death rattle.

A leopard! With fangs clenched on the carcass's throat, the spotted cat dragged its kill to the cluster of trees.

Oja shook with rage, her spear sliding out of her grasp. Fate had cheated her out of her first chance, and now it had done the same a second time. Would it even allow a third? Maybe she should not have insulted her ancestors on her first attempt. Maybe then they would not have sent that leopard to take away what could have been hers.

Tears welled up in Oja's eyes as she picked up her spear. "We must get our kill back."

"No, let the leopard have it," Uru said. "We should head home and pray that our next hunt goes better."

"What? We can't return empty-handed. Our people need meat!"

"Our people also need every one of us to survive," Namak said. "Which is why you're not going to bother that leopard. You'll get yourself hurt, or worse!"

"Why so? There are three of us and only one leopard. We could scare it away without getting one scratch."

Uru shook her head. "Come on, Oja, don't be foolish. The leopard deserves to eat too. Leave it alone."

Oja could not understand why her friends had taken the path of cowardice. Their people were starving. If she could only drive the leopard away from its kill—her kill—it would mean the difference between life and death for what remained of their band.

Maybe she would not stop at merely scaring the cat away. No, she would slay it, too. Oja had never eaten leopard or any other feline's flesh before, but two kills in one day would be more than enough to make up for all the nights her people had slept hungry. She could impress all the other hunters, and possibly even earn their envy. They might even tell stories of her courage around the campfire.

Oja tramped toward the tree in which the leopard was gorging itself on the gazelle. Tilting herself backward as she aimed, she hurled her spear up at the feeding feline.

Again, the obsidian point tasted bark rather than flesh, hitting only the bough supporting the cat and its meal. Startled by the branch's quaking, the leopard glared down at her with flaming yellow eyes, baring its blood-washed fangs as it uttered a defiant hiss.

Oja whipped out her knife from her loincloth thong and brandished it with a yipping battle cry. "Come and get me!"

"Oja, no!" Uru shrieked while running toward her.

With a provoked roar, the leopard sprang off its perch and pounced on Oja, draping itself over her. Its claws sheared her skin as it pinned her to the ground and slashed at her with punitive fury. She swung her knife at the carnivore's cheek, but it ducked its head and bit onto her wrist. Oja thought she could feel the crackle of bone between its fangs as they penetrated her flesh.

As Oja tried to wrestle her hand out of the cat's mouth, Uru stabbed her spear into the cat's flank. It withdrew from Oja with a high-pitched yowl and wheeled around faster than a dust devil, striking at Uru. With four bleeding streaks drawn across her midriff, Uru staggered backward and collapsed.

Another spear soared after the leopard, but the cat jumped out of the missile's path. Namak charged with knife in hand, yelling with bloodlust, until the beast launched itself and collided into her. They wrestled and tumbled together in the grass, Namak's blade slicing through the feline's spotted pelt while its claws raked her.

After forcing herself back onto her feet, Oja threw her knife into the leopard's haunch. The cat yowled a second time, letting go of Namak, and scurried back to the tree where it had perched earlier. It pulled the gazelle carcass off the branch, securing it with its claws and teeth, and retreated deeper into the nearby woods.

Pain from Oja's wounds burned like a brushfire throughout her entire body. Both Uru and Namak stared at her as if they were aiming spears at her own body, their pinpoint eyes already telling Oja what she did not want to hear.

Oja held her head low with a sigh. "I . . . am sorry."

"We should head back to camp," Uru said. "It'll get dark soon."

"So . . . will we hunt again after we've healed?"

"Uru and I will," Namak said. "Next time, however, we won't bring *you* along."

As the sun sank behind the foothills to the west, the sky darkened into violet and then black. The three, all burdened by their wounds, trekked southward at a slow pace across the plains until they spotted the islet of yellow firelight that marked their encampment on the shadowed horizon. The closer they drew to the glowing beacon, the thicker the appetizing odor of meat roasting over the fire grew.

Oja should have felt relief that at least somebody else had found food for their people. Instead, it only compounded her hurt and shame. That could have been *her* gazelle being cooked, and she, Uru, and Namak could have earned all the glory for feeding the band tonight. Who had brought the meat home this time?

The three made their way between the dome-shaped shelters of grass and branches that made up the camp. They walked to the central hearth, around which their people huddled. A triplet of plump hares hung over the flames from a makeshift spit as the band eyed them with hungry anticipation. *A single gazelle would have been more impressive,* Oja thought.

Across the fire from where Oja and her friends stood, her younger brother, Lu, smirked at her, his flint-studded club under his crossed arms.

"Welcome home, Oja," he said. "Would you like a bite of hare?"

"So that's all you've brought home, brother?" Oja asked with a cocked eyebrow.

"At least I brought something back. What about you? You look like you got yourself into a fight!"

Every eye on the band fell on the three huntresses like a flurry of spears being thrown from all directions. Overwhelmed by the gawking attention she was receiving, Oja lowered her head with a sigh while wringing her hands behind her.

"We ran into a leopard," she said. "It . . . took our kill from us."

"And you tried to take it back," Namak added. "You got us all hurt."

Lu widened his sneer. "Isn't that just like my big sister? Getting herself into trouble all the time? At least I was careful out in the bush today. That's why I, unlike you, am the one to feed our people tonight."

"Lu, don't be mean to your sister!" Aukah, their father, spoke next to him. "Your sister and her friends need rest and healing. Show more kindness to her—or be silent."

Oja sat down next to her father, averting her gaze from Lu. He tore off a strip of meat from one of the hares and gave it to her. Despite how much her stomach groaned, she could only nibble on it without savoring its flavor or juiciness as she normally would. Her guilt and disappointment had dulled her tongue's sensitivity to taste.

Aukah laid an arm over his daughter's shoulder, a gentle smile creasing across his wizened gray-bearded face. "You'll feel better in the morning, my child."

Oja could only shrug. It would take more than a single night's sleep to recover from her guilt and humiliation.

CHAPTER TWO
Someone to Hunt With

The last of the stars faded into the sky as it brightened from pure black to dark blue. Oja slumped over the flat top of a rocky pillar that slanted above the edge of the camp. She had not been able to sleep the whole night, and had come to find this position more comfortable than inside her little shelter. She fidgeted with an herb compress her grandfather had strapped to her bitten wrist after the flesh swelled into a hideous dark purple mass which still hurt to touch.

In truth, however, it was not the physical pain that kept her awake all night. It was a wound that pierced deep into her spirit, into her pride.

Next time, we won't bring you along.

Namak's words would not leave Oja alone in peace. They buzzed within her brain like a swarm of bees, stinging her over and over without relent. Namak and Uru had been her two best friends ever since her family joined the band, not long after Oja first learned to walk on her two legs. They, and they alone, played with her throughout her childhood, the three girls chasing each other around the camp before they began pursuing frogs and other small creatures to practice their hunting skills. Now they had given up on her, it seemed, all because of her own foolishness.

She shook her head. She never should have provoked that leopard. Let it eat its kill without disturbance. Maybe not so heroic, but certainly the wiser decision.

Out of the shelter next to Oja's walked Yuke, her mother, who approached the leaning rock and looked up at her daughter, concern shining in her eyes. "What is the matter, my child?"

"Please leave me alone, Mother," Oja said. "I don't deserve your pity."

Yuke did not go away as her daughter had requested. Instead, she climbed onto the rock with a nimbleness defying her advanced age and sat next to Oja, stroking her fluffy black cloud of hair. "All I want is to know what's been gnawing at you all night. I can see the dark bags beneath your eyes."

Oja rubbed her eyelids and blinked. "It's that—Mother, you should know already. I got myself and my two best friends in trouble with that leopard, and now they won't hunt with me anymore. I've brought shame upon myself."

Yuke chuckled, a soothing, calming chuckle. "Oja, we all make mistakes in life. Even your father and I. I think you get your boldness from his side of the family. You should have seen him when we first met."

"Maybe, but my friends aren't willing to put up with my 'boldness' anymore. And what if I get into trouble like that again? The rest of the band will want nothing to do with me, either."

Yuke stared out into the horizon. The sky was starting to turn orange and yellow. She turned to Oja and stroked a tuft of hair from her face. "I don't know what to say about that. But you don't *have* to get yourself in trouble on a hunt again. Why not do what I do instead and dig for roots?"

Oja pouted her lip out in distaste. When she was a little girl, she had spent hours digging beside her mother alongside the other children and elders in the band. The miserable, exhausting chore always wore out her hands and layered her limbs with dust. While biting down on the tubers they excavated may provide welcome moisture on a hot and dry day, it could never match a succulent, tangy morsel of meat in deliciousness.

"Why would I do *that*?" Oja said. "I am not a child anymore, nor am I old like you. I should be able to hunt like any woman my age! Or man!"

"I see." Yuke rubbed her short gray-speckled hair, thinking of another way. "Say, if you must hunt, why don't you hunt beside your brother instead of your friends? He could learn from you."

"Oh, Mother, you know Lu wouldn't want me around."

"Why not? I've only ever seen him go out with his friend Tukar. They can't have a problem with a third hunter helping them."

Oja shrugged her shoulders. "Fair enough."

"Whatever you choose to do, my child, you should wait until that swelling in your wrist goes away." Yuke tapped a finger on her daughter's compress. "That must hurt like an evil spirit."

"Oh, it'll get better soon. At least no bones were broken."

"If you say so."

The sun soared over the earth from east to west, yielding the heavens to the moon and stars after it sank. Once the sun returned from its nightly slumber, everyone in the band voted to leave camp, having eaten all the tubers and chased off all the game in the area. They put out the fire with scoops of dirt, kicked down their shelters, and walked away without looking back at what had taken hours to set up.

Such was the way of the people who had roamed the plains since time immemorial. Nobody could stay in a camp forever, for that was not the way of the people of the plains. Much as the herds always migrated between pastures and waterholes, with predators always prowling close by, so did the people. Crafty and clever as they may have been, human beings were little more than a special breed of animal, no less so than the zebra, the lion, or the baboon.

After a morning and midday spent trekking across the rolling grasslands together, the people stopped by a waterhole to slake their thirst and wash themselves. They cleaned the dust off their skin while relishing the relief from the heat. Afterward, the band's strong young men gathered branches and assembled them into arching frameworks on which the women and elders draped grass and leaves, thus completing the new camp's shelters.

Meanwhile, the boys Lu and Tukar were responsible for setting up the night's hearth. First Tukar laid down a pile of grassy tinder in the center of the camp, with a thicker log laying on top. Then Lu knelt by this pile and used his hands to drill a stick spindle into the log. He started to summon smoke from the friction between the wood pieces.

"Lu?"

He grumbled in irritation. "Can it wait?"

"Don't be rude to your own sister like that," Oja retorted. "I only wanted to ask one thing. Next time you and your friend are ready to go hunting, can I go with you?"

Lu let go of his spindle. He stared at her, his eyes narrowed. "You must have gone crazy. After what you did with that leopard on your last hunt, or what that leopard did to *you,* you want *me* to bring you along? You'll get us all killed!"

Tukar grinned wide, exposing the gap in his front teeth where an incisor had been knocked out in a brawl some time ago. His eyes ran up and down the curves of Oja's figure as he smacked his lips. "Oh, I wouldn't mind her coming with us. If you don't mind me saying, Lu, your sister doesn't look bad at all."

Oja's nose wrinkled as if she had smelled freshly dropped dung. Somehow the prospect of hunting beside Lu and Tukar in place of her friends did not appeal as much anymore. Especially not if Tukar, that lanky jackal of a boy, was going to regard her as many men would regard a comely young woman.

She took a step back. "On second thought, Lu, maybe it should be you and I hunting by ourselves."

"What's the matter, sister?" Lu asked with a snicker. "Don't want my longtime friend hunting by your side?"

"Not if he's going to . . . you know . . ."

"Oh, come on, you women scare too easily," Tukar said. "You know I meant no insult to you. Besides, if I were, uh, taller and stronger, you wouldn't mind at all."

Oja's distaste sizzled into anger. She wished she had her butchering knife on her. "I couldn't care less how handsome you are, Tukar. Back off or I will slap your cheek off your skull!"

Lu stood up and jumped between her and his friend, arms crossed. "That is enough. Tukar has been my friend as long as Uru and Namak have been yours. I will never hunt without him. And if that means you will never hunt with us together, then so be it."

"Then fine!"

Oja stormed away from her brother and retreated into the shelter she had claimed for herself. She dropped herself onto the floor of trampled grass, wrapped her arms around her legs, and stewed in silence. Not even the shade offered by the shelter's ceiling could cool her temper.

Something touched her on the back. A startled Oja spun around on her bottom. "What is it?"

Yuke finished stepping inside and pinched between her fingers a fat yam she had excavated while the shelters were being raised. "I heard your offer to hunt with Lu didn't go over so well."

"You heard right. So what should I do, Mother?"

"Well, like I said yesterday, you could always dig with us instead. You don't *have* to go hunting with anyone."

Oja's face lit up with an idea that had percolated in her brain all day. "That's it! I'll go hunting by myself then."

"What? No! You know it's too dangerous to go out into the bush alone."

"Oh, I won't go after anything *big*, Mother. Only after prey I can kill with one spear. But, if the leopard can hunt all by itself, why can't I?"

"You are not a leopard, Oja! Were you not almost killed by one? What makes you think you can survive out there on your own?"

"Trust me, I can. I won't make the same mistake again."

"Forget it. I won't let you go alone. Neither will your father nor anyone else in the band allow such a thing." Yuke's stern look melted into a smile as she held the yam closer to her daughter. "Promise me you'll stay at camp where you will be safe, my child."

Oja accepted the yam and bit into it, enjoying its sweet juices. "I promise, Mother. That I swear by all our ancestors."

"Thank you, then."

Yuke patted her daughter's hair. That made Oja feel a faint pang of guilt for not just speaking the truth.

CHAPTER THREE
The Rhino and the Rapids

Oja retired to sleep on the very cusp of sundown, earlier than the rest of the band. When asked why she was not going to listen to campfire stories, she told her family that she had worn herself out after a busy day's work, and also that her wounded wrist still needed as much rest as she could make for it. These were not complete lies, but still only half of the truth. The main reason Oja curled down on her shelter's floor so early was to get up before everyone else.

Which she did. The sky was still dark across its entire breadth when she crawled out of her shelter, the waning crescent of the moon giving off just enough light for her to make out the contours of the camp's structures and the savanna beyond. With a silent, stealth imitation of a stalking wildcat, Oja crept over to the shelter to the right of her own, inside of which her mother and father lay together in a tender embrace.

She was thankful that her father's snoring, as loud as a crocodile's bellowing growl, would mask any sound she might make.

The glassy gleam of an obsidian point above the floor marked Aukah's hunting spear as it leaned against the shelter's branch framework. In the handful of days that had passed since the ill-fated hunt with her friends, Oja had not found time to make another spear after losing hers in the incident with the leopard. Never in her life had she taken another person's possessions, and she wanted to steal from her own family less than anyone else in the band. But how could she hunt this morning if she did not have a worthy weapon?

Please forgive me, beloved Father, Oja begged in her mind as she plucked the spear up from its resting place. *And forgive me too, Mother, for breaking my promise.*

Now armed, she snuck back out of the shelter and paused to scan the camp around her. No one else was out. The fire Lu made the past evening lay dead in a pile of ash and burnt tinder. It occurred to her nothing would discourage a leopard, lions, or hyenas from ambushing the camp while its people still slept. She lost an uncle to such an attack a couple of rainy seasons ago. If such flesh-eaters were on their way, she might encounter them while she was out in the bush, and then she could fight them off before they had a chance to hurt any of her people. The whole band would shower her with gratitude for that. Even Uru and Namak might reconsider letting her hunt with them!

As it stood, nothing lurked around the camp. The crickets chirped and a grass owl screeched from its perch on a nearby marula tree, but no creature purred, growled, or even rustled the grass and bushes. It was as close to tranquil as a night on the savanna could get.

Oja tightened her grip on the spear and stole past the outermost shelters. She skirted the waterhole next to the camp and then followed the moon as it drifted between the stars high over the plains. As she jogged, she kept eyes and ears open with full alertness in all directions, careful to breathe only through her nose so that her panting did not spook potential prey.

A pale speck flashed through the underbrush to her right. Lowering her torso beneath the tips of the tall grass, Oja tiptoed to the spot of the sudden movement. She crouched to the ground and noted the faint, elongated paw prints of a running hare. Oja's first impulse was to ignore it and continue. A single hare would produce even less meat than what Lu brought to camp the other day.

Yet, had she not promised her mother that she would not go after anything large and dangerous when hunting by herself? She had broken one promise already; two would be worse. For all she knew, she might not find a more worthy quarry the rest of the day. One hare, though unimpressive, would be better than coming back with empty hands. At least then she would have something to make up for taking her father's spear and running away from camp so early in the morning.

She stalked the path of tracks that led southward, a sliver of indigo sky now emergent over the dark horizon to her left. At the same time, the cool nocturnal air began to give way to the warmth of daybreak, but perspiration drenched Oja after so much running. She hoped to catch the hare before the sun reached its sizzling midday apex, but she could not count on it.

Again, a tiny gray-brown blur shot across the savanna. It halted to stand upright on a rock, its long ears erect and twitching. Kneeling to the ground, Oja stretched her spear-arm back and aimed at the hare, clenching her hand on the shaft, grasping it firmly. She licked her lips. After treating her with such unforgiving cruelty on the last hunt, today's fate was showing kindness as if to make up for it.

The moment Oja let her spear fly, the hare hopped back into cover. The spear struck rock before dropping to the ground.

She cursed with frustration. *Not again!*

After picking up her weapon, she sprinted after the hare as it bounded over the grassland. The world blurred together on both sides between her and her quarry, a breeze whistling past her. Driven by desperation as much as hunger, Oja recognized but otherwise paid no heed to the aching of her legs while she ran.

The chase led them to a long, deep ravine bridged by a slender fallen log. The hare crossed over it in a few leaps. When Oja set her lead foot on the log, it cracked under her weight and dropped into the ravine's depths. She had neither the time nor desire to walk around the winding gorge. Even if she did, she would have lost her prey anyway. Grumbling under her breath, she gave up the pursuit and walked away.

There needed to be something else she could hunt between now and the scorching midday. Something she could bring down alone and yet provide enough meat for the band. Surveying the plain around her several times, she found nothing like the wild game she sought. There were only grass, trees, and a littering of rocky outcrops as far as she could see. She growled and kicked a large boulder in a fit of frustrated rage.

To her surprise, her foot bounced off not a surface of hard stone but rather soft, wrinkled flesh. The sides of the big "rock" swelled and sank like the belly of a massive animal as it slowly rose onto four stumpy legs. Its low-slung head bore two curved horns atop its snout, the front horn longer and sharper than the rear. It squinted at Oja with beady eyes, its snort expressing as much irritation as the look it was giving her.

She was petrified, the shock close to overwhelming. The rhinoceros pawed the ground with its three-toed foreleg and held its head low, with its horns aimed straight at her. Pointing her own weapon at the behemoth, Oja took one step back and then another, trying not to startle the animal with any sudden movements.

After emitting a nasal bray, the rhino exploded into a gallop at a speed that belied its bulk. Oja raced to the nearest acacia tree, holding the shaft of the spear between her teeth. She jumped, grabbing the lowest branch. As she hauled herself off the earth, the brute's horns slashed the air beneath her. She hugged the tree's trunk with quaking limbs until the rhinoceros lumbered off with a disappointed grunt.

Her heart pounded in a frenzy matching the rhino's stomping feet. That was one creature of the savanna she would not bother again. Once he forgot about her and cleared the area, she would hurry away as far as she could from its grazing grounds and continue her hunt elsewhere.

Or would she? She'd had no luck finding the small prey she sought. The rhino was not small by any means, but it was still a body of meat. If Oja could carve out only one of its thickset legs and bring it back to camp . . . *no, what a foolish thought!* She shook her head repeatedly, trying to get the notion out of her head. Her spear would not bring down a full-grown rhino by itself. Or even come close.

Unless I were to chuck it right into its little brain . . .

After the rhino wandered a small distance away, Oja stood up on the acacia bough and aligned the point of her spear with the beast's head. Under her breath, she murmured a prayer to her ancestors that her weapon would fly true and bring down something for once. She had missed enough times—and she would not do so again.

She flung the spear with a warlike yipping cry. It hit the rhino on the rear of its skull, but the mighty horned herbivore did not topple over in death. Instead, it wheeled around and hurtled into the acacia tree, shaking it fiercely. Only by grabbing onto another branch above her was Oja able to prevent herself from falling off.

Twice again the infuriated rhino rammed the tree. Oja's fingers slipped off, and she fell.

She did not hit solid earth within an instant as she had expected. Instead, she plummeted through whistling air, the rugged stone face of a cliff shooting up over her and spinning as her body twirled. That tree had stood above the edge of a cliff! How could she have missed that? Instead of being gored by a rhinoceros, she was now going to crash down to her death . . .

Her mother had been right. It was too dangerous for a human to hunt alone. Had Oja brought someone with her—anyone—they would have watched out for her and kept her from making such foolish mistakes. Because she had chosen to hunt by herself, though, she would die before seeing her twenty-second rainy season.

She landed at last, but not with a splat upon hard earth. Instead, she plunged into cold, churning white water.

Before she could float back to the surface, the current shoved Oja into a rock. She grabbed it with her arms and pushed herself up to take a breath, but the next moment, the raging river plucked her off her purchase and tossed her about like a hunting dog thrashing a piece of meat in its mouth. It flung her up into the air, pressed her back down into its depths, and threw her into more rocks that scraped and cut at her skin. Oja's blood began dyeing the frothing white foam pink.

Ahead of her, the water ended before the horizon the way land would cease at the lip of a cliff. The current gained greater strength, dragging her to the edge even as she waved her arms and kicked her legs in a frantic effort to swim to safety. No matter how hard she tried, she was no match for its power and speed.

All she could do was succumb to the river's pull and fall alongside the torrent of water that roared over the edge . . .

CHAPTER FOUR
Stranded

Aukah snapped out of his dreams when he felt a pair of hands shake his shoulder.

"Aukah, what happened to your spear?" he heard Yuke ask.

He opened his eyes and noticed the spear's absence inside their shelter. Underneath where it had lain, a faint line of footprints ran back and forth on the dusty floor. Somebody snuck into the shelter to take his spear . . . who?

Aukah shot up from rest and out of the shelter into the dawn air. In his loudest voice, he roared, "Who took my spear last night?"

Lu was the first to rise, his eyes still half-shut. "What happened, Father?"

"Somebody went into my shelter last night and took my spear. Was it you?"

"No. Why would I do such a thing?"

Aukah turned toward Oja's shelter next. "Then was it you, Oja! Oja?"

He heard nothing. Nor did she emerge into view as her brother had. Walking toward her shelter, Aukah peeked inside it.

She was gone.

"Oja?" Aukah shouted outside the shelter between cupped hands. "Oja, where are you?"

No answer.

The rest of the camp started to stir, people coming out to stand all around Aukah, curious as to what the commotion was about.

"Have any of you seen Oja?" Aukah asked his gathering audience. "Uru, Namak, do you know where she went?"

Her two friends shook their heads with blank looks in their eyes.

"I believe I know what she's done," Yuke said. "She told me she wanted to hunt by herself since nobody else would go with her. I told her not to do it, but . . ."

"So she is the one who took my spear!" Aukah said. "But why? This isn't like her at all!"

Lu crossed his arms, his smirk smug. "I don't know about that, Father. You know she always acts before she thinks."

Namak nodded in agreement. "Believe me, that's a gentle way of putting it."

Uru stared at the ground, fidgeting with her hands behind her back. "To tell you the truth, father of Oja, I believe the fault is ours. Namak and I were the ones who told her we would not let her hunt with us anymore. No wonder she chose to go out on her own."

"It wasn't all your fault, Uru," Tukar said as he stood beside Lu. "I acted, let's say, too hastily toward Oja when she offered to hunt with me and Lu. Had I treated her better, she wouldn't have run off like this."

"Bah, I wouldn't have trusted her with us anyway," Lu said.

"Lu! Show more respect toward your sister," Aukah said. "Anyway, no matter who wants to take the blame, it won't change that my daughter is gone. Uru, Namak, could you track her down and bring her back?"

"We will do what we can," Uru answered.

Namak bit her lip for a quick moment before nodding. "As much as I don't like to have to get Oja out of trouble again, she does need us this time."

Aukah spread his arms wide open and hugged the two women together. "Then I owe you two my thanks."

Oja splashed into another body of water. The bottom of the falls raged with the same frothing turbulence as the rapids before it, washing over more rocks that further battered and scratched her. She drifted with the current, which finally slowed into a gentler flow that carried her floating body into a broader stretch of river. It did not run within a narrow ravine of cliffs as before, but was edged with flat banks of gravel that eventually gave way to thick hedges of papyrus reeds.

Once the current had waned enough to not overpower her anymore, Oja swam with fanning strokes of her arms to the river's edge and climbed through the reeds onto the muddy bank. Her body dripped water, as well as blood from various cuts and scrapes, her hide garments clinging onto her skin. After vomiting a mouthful of river water, she shook herself dry like a wet hunting dog and wrung her hair tight.

At least, with the sun high enough in the sky, it was pleasantly balmy. She did not want to imagine how much she would have shivered had it still been dark out!

Alongside the riverbank's far boundary, she noticed a bushy woodland of trees that commonly grew alongside large bodies of water. A troop of vervet monkeys gawked at her with their reddish-brown eyes from atop one of the trees, chirping and chattering between themselves. Hoping that the primates' gaze was one of curiosity rather than lechery, Oja turned her back toward them and looked across the river to the north.

Beyond the trees on the opposite bank, she spotted a wall of craggy rock like the one she had tumbled into the rapids from. She concluded the plains she and her people roamed must lay on the upper surface of whatever expanse of land terminated at the lip of those cliffs. In which case, Oja would have descended into another, lower level of the world, separated by sheer elevation from the one she had known all her life.

She studied the cliffs further. Was there a passage between them? Were they scalable at all? She looked desperately, realizing if she couldn't find a way up, she would be unable to return to her band, and her family. Her spirits waned as she kept searching. She had succeeded only in stranding herself from everyone she knew.

And she could blame nobody else but herself.

Her stomach purred with vibrating hunger. She should not have wasted her spear—her father's spear—on that rhinoceros. Not only would it come in handy for hunting right now, but she could use its stone point to dig up tubers, as much as she detested that chore. As it was, there were unlikely to be many trees or plants bearing fruit at this time of year, since it was still the dry season. How could she find or hunt for anything to eat while all her cuts and bruises from the rhino and the rapids burdened her?

The monkeys were still gawking at her from up in the trees. Could she eat one of them? She had never eaten vervet monkey before, but she had eaten baboon once, and it did not bother her palate, from what she remembered. It wouldn't take much to take out one of these little primates. She wouldn't even need a spear.

Oja picked up a rock as big as her fist. "Forgive me, monkey, but I must eat."

She released the stone at the full troop as if it were a spear. They leaped across the high branches, hooting, their cries panicked, but her rudimentary missile missed. It bounced off the tree on which they had perched and dropped harmlessly to the ground. *What is wrong with my throwing ability? I can't even hit my target with a simple stone, never mind a spear!*

She knew she could not give up. Resigning herself to starvation and death would extinguish even the faintest hope of reuniting with the band. She would never see her family again. *No*, she vowed, *I must survive out here.*

After retrieving the rock she had thrown, Oja entered the woodland beyond the riverbank, following the direction the monkey troop took. As she glided between the trees through the undergrowth of saplings, shrubs, and high grass, she scoured the overhanging canopy of leaves and twisted boughs. Several times, she caught fleeting glimpses of smaller creatures, such as scurrying bush squirrels or fluttering birds, but she knew she had an even smaller chance of catching these fast, fleeting beings than she did the monkeys.

A noisome odor stung her nostrils. She stopped. Sniffing the air some more, Oja identified the sharp smell of blood. Somewhere nearby lay the carcass of an animal, which would at least save her the effort of having to kill it. For once, fate had shown at least the most basic kindness!

After deducing where the carrion scent carried from, she followed it by jogging eagerly through the woods. As the scent grew stronger in her nose, she could hear the buzzing of flies growing louder and clearer as well. Her legs carried her faster and faster. Her excitement was building.

Finally, she came upon the fallen creature. A waterbuck. The large antelope's flank had been torn open, intestines and other organs spilling out of its splintered rib cage. Under most circumstances, the gore-swathed sight would have repulsed Oja, but not now. Instead, she eyed this mass of flesh with the slavering hunger of a jackal. Now all she needed was something to cut off slivers of meat. Perhaps she could break the rock in half and use the edge of one piece to saw off the meat. Or maybe . . .

Her knife! She rubbed over her right hip and found it still tucked under the thong of her loincloth. How could she have overlooked it? How did it survive the tossing and turning of the river? Grateful she had somehow kept it attached after everything she had endured that morning, she took out the knife, tossed away the rock, and started slicing meat from one of the waterbuck's forelegs.

She had almost gathered what she needed when a gust of hot, moist air brushed onto her forehead. Her legs shuddering, she tilted her head up to find herself looking into the flaming amber eyes of a lion. The massive, dark-maned cat's fangs glistened wet with drool as it bared them with a threatening growl.

Oja had no intention of provoking the mightiest predator of the savanna. Clenching the meat she'd harvested in a tight fist, she stepped back from the carcass until she was a safe distance away and then sprinted with the speed of a fleeing gazelle, leaving the lion to devour what she had found, uncontested.

At least, by the mercy of her ancestors, she had collected enough food to last the remainder of the day. Would she be so lucky the rest of her time in this lowland place, cut off from her people, not knowing if she would ever see them again?

CHAPTER FIVE
The White Outcast

After a thorough search of the ground outside their encampment, Uru and Namak found the slender footprints of a young woman trailing southward, the heels pointing toward Aukah's shelter. This did not prove beyond doubt that Oja laid those tracks, but neither had they noticed or heard of any other woman leaving the camp overnight. The prints they found left crisp edges with little wear, which their practiced eyes told them was evidence that the walker had left not long ago.

Morning brightened toward midday as the two women pursued the trail across the savanna. At one point, Namak observed that the tinier tracks of a hare intersected the path laid by Oja, the latter then angling to run parallel to the former. A sure sign Oja had gone after the hare upon spotting it. Further following of the twin trails brought the trackers to the edge of a ravine where the hare's tracks ended, Oja's tracks turned away.

"You think Oja speared the hare here?" Uru asked.

Namak brushed her hand through the grass over the very end of the hare's trail. "I don't see any blood. Or any imprint the body would have left. Seems to me the hare simply fell into the gorge. Or crossed it somehow."

She peered down the ravine and noted the fallen, halfway-splintered log at the bottom. Whether that log had been there before, or rolled over after the hare had run across it to the other side, Namak could not know for sure.

"Our poor friend never seems to have any luck, does she?" Uru said.

Namak clicked her tongue against her palate twice. "She never was that great with aim."

They continued to follow Oja's trail.

It was not long before they found the tracks bouncing off another stream of much wider, three-toed impressions. Their hearts sank within their breasts. They knew these as the distinctive prints of a rhinoceros, the most massive animal of the savanna after the elephant. And the rhino tracks had turned . . . likely to chase Oja..

"She couldn't have . . ." Namak said under her breath.

She spotted a spear resting in the grass to the side. She picked it up and ran her finger over the dried blood that stained its obsidian head just below where the very tip had been fractured off. If Oja had thrown this at the rhino, she would have been even more foolish than Namak expected. Was there no end to their friend's arrogance?

Meanwhile, Uru traced Oja and the rhino's trails to an acacia tree leaning over where the earth dropped off another cliff. Although the rhino tracks then turned away from the tree, Oja's had not. Instead, her trail ended at the tree's roots, like she had disappeared from existence from that spot.

Maybe Oja climbed up the tree to escape the charging rhino. That would make sense. But why hadn't she come down? No matter how meticulously Uru searched the grass and dirt surrounding the acacia tree, she could not find any more footprints.

Uru looked up at the tree again. The lowest-hanging branch appeared to have broken off. It could not have happened long ago, as the remaining stump was bleeding fluid sap as if a wound in flesh. Was this the branch Oja climbed? If her weight broke it underneath, would that mean . . .

Far below the cliff, half-shrouded by a layer of white mist, rapids surged within a wider canyon. *No, it could not be true*, Uru thought. Oja could not have fallen down there. If so, there could be no way she survived.

Uru buried her face in her hands and began to weep.

"What's the matter—" Namak started to ask.

"She's gone," Uru said through her tears. "Our friend Oja is gone."

"How so?"

Uru pointed down the cliff. "She must have fallen into those rapids down there. If the fall didn't kill her already, those waters sure would have."

"I don't think we know that for sure. Some people are tougher than others, or their ancestors are looking out for them. All I'm saying is, there's a chance she could still be alive."

Uru looked up, her eyes filled with tears. "Really? Even if that were so, we have no idea where she could have been carried to. She's lost to us, maybe forever."

Namak sighed. "You're right. Ooh, that poor, stupid girl! Her family will be crushed by grief. And all because she had to go her own way!"

"May her ancestors keep watch over her, regardless."

After giving the rapids one last look, their hearts weighing heavy, both of the women Oja knew as friends headed back to their people's camp.

Oja found a large, flat table of granite with one corner projecting into the river. An ideal spot for camp. It rose high enough to provide her with an extensive vantage over both river and bank, allowing her to spot potential predators. Yet at the same time it was just low enough to climb onto, thanks to a single raised step. Furthermore, it provided an obvious landmark she could remember whenever she wandered the area.

She harvested a bundle of dry sticks and grass from the woods, laid them on the center of the rock's surface, and struck together two chunks of flint until sparks shot down to produce a small flame. It was not the exact fire-starting technique her brother would use back at camp, when he rubbed a spindle over a log amid the kindle, but rather one Oja had seen her mother use before. It mattered not which technique she used; each obtained the same result.

After making her fire, she roasted a few scraps of waterbuck meat over it and ate them for her midday meal. It had been a long time since she had eaten meat from any type of antelope, so she relished its tangy, succulent flavor. She hid the remainder of the meat by placing a smaller boulder over it.

After filling her stomach, Oja's next task was to make a spear of her own. The carcasses of dead animals would be too hard for her to find for the rest of the dry season, however long it would continue to last. She would have to kill food for herself, and as previous experience showed, throwing stones would not be enough.

Creating the spear shaft proved simple enough. All she had to do was find a long, slender branch in the nearby woods and whittle off any bumps or other protrusions with her knife. Then she heated her stick and shaped it further. Now that she had her shaft, it was time to tip it off with the killing point.

So far, she had not spotted any obsidian for spearheads lying around. Normally her people would obtain that sharp, glassy rock through trade with the hill-dwellers of the far west. Now, though, she would have to content herself with a common piece of flint, like the blade of her knife.

Oja browsed the shore of the river near her makeshift camp for nodules of flint worthy of a spearhead. This proved more difficult than expected. While there were innumerable stones buried within the riverbank, far rarer were specimens of flint of suitable size or shape. More than once, she plunged her fingers into the sediment to pluck out a fragment of rock that seemed ideal at first glance, only to find that it was disappointingly small or the wrong kind of rock.

Something rustled in the distant bushes. Oja stilled herself and stared at the undergrowth alongside the riverbank. The shadows cast by the trees had turned blacker, a sign the day was giving way to evening. Holding her hand over her knife's handle, Oja waited for whatever disturbed the vegetation to reveal itself.

Nothing. She shrugged and resumed foraging for flint.

"What are you searching for, stranger?"

The voice rang louder than the roar of a leopard. She spun on her heels, her knife drawn. A man crouched on her rock platform, suspiciously close to where she had hidden her meat. It was a young man, about Lu's age, unlike anyone from her band. His skin glowed like a ghost from the light of the sunset, white as mountaintop snow rather than black like most people. His bushy hair and beard cast a pale yellow color. With eyes blue as a midday sky, he looked back at Oja with pinkish-red lips parted into a toothy smile.

Oja leaped back with a startled yelp. "You're . . . you're . . . who . . . what are you?"

"Oh, don't mind me," the man said. "I can't help that I was born white."

"But . . . why?"

"Why? All I know is that my mother told me a wicked spirit turned me white when I was still in her womb. That's what happens to all children who are born like me . . . different, isn't it?" The man hopped off the rock and extended a hand to Oja, still smiling with a child's innocence. "By the way, I am called Urjah."

After a moment's hesitation, Oja put away her knife and touched the man's fingertips with her own. Inspecting her hands afterward, she was surprised to find none of his whiteness had rubbed onto her like body paint.

"Don't worry, I won't hurt you," Urjah said. "I simply don't see anyone else wandering into my foraging ground these days."

"You don't have a band of your own?" Oja asked.

"A 'band' . . . oh, you're one of those people who wander all over the plains! Well, my family didn't come from that. They came from this village . . . you know what a village is, don't you?"

"I've . . . heard of them. It's a band of people who build a big camp in one place and then live their whole lives in it . . ."

"Yes, that's it. You find a lot of them alongside rivers, where they can fish all year long instead of having to chase game everywhere like your people do. Anyway, my family's village was a few days' walk downstream from here, but they left because . . ."

Urjah paused to turn his back and gaze in a direction parallel to the river's course, as if pining for the village of his ancestors.

She laid her hand on his shoulder. "Because of what?"

"Because they had me. It was either leave, or have me put to death because I was born with this curse. So I've spent my whole life with my family out here in the bush. And ever since both my mother and father left for their ancestors several rains ago, I've been on my own."

Moisture swelled and glistened in Urjah's eyes until he wiped it away with his arm. Oja's heart melted within her chest for this poor man, who had been stranded like herself in this vast, hostile wilderness.

She reached under the rock platform to where she had hidden her saved meat and offered a handful of it to the white-skinned outcast. "You won't be alone anymore. Want to share this with me tonight?"

The frown on Urjah's face vanished, giving way to his earlier grin. "Sure! But not out here. I have a little home deeper in the woods where we can eat. Has a shelter and everything."

"Everything? You wouldn't happen to have a spare spear or two, would you?"

Urjah nodded. "I have one I use for fishing. But why would a woman like you need a spear?"

Oja crossed her arms and cocked an eyebrow. "Why wouldn't I? I need it to hunt, fish, and defend myself, same as you."

"A woman . . . hunting and fishing." Urjah fluttered his eyelids as if he didn't believe her. "I guess women of the plains are different from those of the river."

"How so?"

"Well, um . . . never mind. Let's head over to my hut already, shall we?"

Oja narrowed her eyes at Urjah, shaking her head. This man was strange in more ways than skin color alone. If women could not hunt among his people, what were they supposed to do? And why weren't they able to hunt, anyway? Were women from the river villages somehow weaker or less capable than their counterparts of the plains?

She shook her head, dismissing the thought. Even if his view of women was odd, Urjah was the only other human Oja had seen in this new land. She might as well appreciate his company if she was to spend the rest of her life here.

Oja climbed onto the rocky table and stamped out her campfire. She picked up the shaft of her unfinished spear, along with the remaining waterbuck meat, and followed Urjah into the trees along the bank.

After a brief stroll through the woodland south of the river, they arrived at a grassy glade. Her eyes fell onto a construction well over twice the size of any of the shelters Oja's people built. This was not simply a larger variation of those temporary dwellings, however. Its curved walls were built of sticks woven together like a basket, supporting a cone of thatch for a roof. Outside this building's entrance crackled a cooking fire like the one she had made earlier, but with a wooden spit mounted above it.

"Welcome to my humble home," Urjah said.

"Whoa, did you build this by yourself?" Oja asked.

"No, my father did. But I've been keeping it standing ever since."

He went into the hut and came back with what Oja took to be a basket at first. She looked more closely, and the sight surprised her: this basket was made not of plant fibers but of a hard, earthy brown substance with zigzagging red-and-white stripes painted on it. And it was a vessel, not a basket.

Inside was a reddish-orange powder. "This is something that'll spice up the meat," Urjah explained.

Oja tapped the edge of the bowl. "What is this . . . basket . . . made of?"

"You mean the bowl? Dried clay, made by my mother. She was quite good with clay."

"You know how to make things out of clay yourself?"

Urjah chuckled. "Nope. That's women's work. Pity you don't seem to know how to do it yourself. Then I would have a good use for you."

Oja snorted, her mouth pulled wide into a grimacing frown. "Oh, so that's what women do among your people instead of hunting!"

"Not only that. You're also good for gathering tubers and berries, cooking . . . and, of course, raising the children."

"Ugh! Well, since you've done so well for yourself for so long out here without a woman, surely you will be able to cook the meat tonight?"

Oja flung her scraps of waterbuck meat at Urjah. He gawked at her while scratching his hair with a confused grunt.

When she peered into his eyes, Oja's anger was doused by a pint of pity. The man truly had never met a woman of the plains before. For that matter, if his parents had left their riverside community after birthing him, he might never have known or even seen any woman other than his own mother. Never could he have known better.

She picked up the meat at his feet. "Alright, I'll cook it."

"No, let me," Urjah said. "Why don't you check out the inside of my hut in the meantime? You will find my spear in there, if that's what you're interested in."

As he attended to the food and the fire, Oja did as he suggested and walked into the hut, ducking her head beneath its branch lintel. Leaning against the wall at its back was a spear with a sharp, barbed head of bone hafted to it, with a flint-and-bone axe resting alongside it. These did not pique her curiosity as much as two more objects next to them. The first was a tall, cylindrical container of tanned hide that carried over a dozen little shafts, with a long strap sewn onto its side. The second article of interest was a slender, curved limb of wood with a string of twisted animal gut connecting its ends.

Oja tiptoed toward the sack of shafts and pinched one out. Tipped with a bone point at one end, it resembled a miniature spear. But what could it kill when thrown? Did these shafts somehow have a relationship to the piece of wood with the string attached to its ends? Or was their only thing in common the unfamiliarity to her?

"Urjah, what's this piece of wood with a string on it for?" Oja called out from inside the hut.

"Oh, the bow? It's another hunting tool of mine," Urjah replied. "Shouldn't be of your concern, really. It requires a man's strength to use best."

Oja suppressed a quick flashing temptation to prick her host in the backside with his own spear. "Come on, can't a woman use it at all? And how, by the ancestors, could you use it to kill prey anyway?"

"Alright, if you insist, I'll show you tomorrow."

"That's more like it."

Oja came out of the hut to sit opposite Urjah at the campfire and watch the meat cook. His eyes kept bouncing between their roasting dinner and her, a grin on his face that almost resembled how Tukar had ogled her the day before. Every time she caught him doing that, Urjah would turn his head away as if in shame.

"You like looking at me, don't you?" Oja asked.

Urjah's cheeks blushed a light pink. "It's only that I've never known a woman other than my own mother. But you aren't like her, in many ways. No, you are as different from her as the leopard is to the gazelle."

His choice of words brought to mind Oja's big incident, a painful twinge to her memory. "Sounds like it might be true."

Urjah paused for a brief moment. "If you don't mind me asking, Oja . . . would you like to be my woman? We could raise a family of our own out here, all by ourselves. Maybe even build a whole village, if more people come to join us."

"No, you are too young and skinny for me, even if you weren't born white. But we can still live together as friends."

Oja reached around the fire to touch his wrist with a gentle beam. At first, Urjah pouted his lower lip, but then returned the gesture by placing his own hand on her wrist.

"Then it is enough that we shall be friends," he said.

CHAPTER SIX
Old Wounded

Aukah spent the whole day beneath the shade of a stout old baobab tree on the camp's edge, his watchful gaze never leaving the southern horizon in which Uru and Namak had disappeared. Every few hours, Yuke walked over with a full waterskin and a morsel of yam, but he touched neither. Not even the smallest pleasures could lure him away from his worries for even a few seconds.

As the sun descended, he spotted a pair of black dots rising on the horizon. They grew larger . . . humans, walking . . . his daughter's two best friends, drawing nearer. He breathed a sigh of relief. *They're back.* But then he stopped his next breath. The coveted third figure Aukah anticipated seeing most of all was not alongside them. His worst fears.

Uru and Namak stopped before him without speaking any words. Their lowered heads said everything.

"You never found her, did you?" Aukah said.

Namak held up a spear Aukah recognized as his own, despite the blood-stained and broken tip. She placed it in his hands. "Only this."

"We think she fell off a cliff into a river of rapids," Uru said. "I am sorry to say this, but she might as well have passed on to rejoin her ancestors."

Their report choked Aukah too much for him to say a word in reply. This was all his fault, his and Yuke's. They should have taught

Oja to restrain herself and show more caution, to never leave sight of her companions while out in the bush. The girl's spirit, so much like his own in youth, had drawn her away from him . . . and everything else in this world.

The spear in his hands would not be his any longer. When the time came for the band to dig a grave for Oja and mourn her passing, he would bury it where her body would have lain. It mattered not that she had taken the spear from him. Her spirit, as it floated among those of all generations before her, would respect the gift.

Oja's eyelids parted to a bright golden wave of sunlight pouring through the hut's entryway. Thus awakened, she lifted her back off the cheetah-hide blanket Urjah had provided her and stretched her forelimbs upward while taking in a deep yawn. There still lingered within her mouth the hot, spicy aftertaste from the orange powder he had applied to their meal last night. Unfamiliar as the flavor was, it was not an unpleasant one, yet it did leave her feeling a bit thirsty.

Her eyes dug around the hut in search of a waterskin, like those her people carried on long journeys between waterholes. She found one hanging from a post inserted into the wall and sampled its contents with a sip, but then spat it out. The water was too stale for her liking.

Urjah, who lay curled up on his own blanket next to her, rose up at last. "Are you alright, Oja?"

"You need to refill this," she said with a shake of the waterskin. "The water's gone bad."

"Good thing you reminded me. We can do that while I show you how to use the bow."

After picking up his bow and slinging the sack of little spears around his torso, Urjah waved for Oja to follow him out of the hut. Together they walked through the woodland until they returned to the riverbank, where Oja had set up her campfire on the table of rock the previous day. A few yards downriver, a herd of waterbuck drank, living brethren of the one whose carcass she had scavenged.

"Good thing they showed up," Urjah said. "We can practice on real prey after I show you how to use the bow. What would you say to that?"

Oja was occupied with dumping out the stale water from the waterskin and filling it up again from the river. She took a swig, savoring the water's sweeter, fresher taste, and then splashed it onto her face for relief against the morning's building heat. Thus satiated, she climbed onto the big flat rock where Urjah stood.

He took out one of the little spears from its container. "We call this an arrow, and the thing we hold them in is a quiver. If you look closely at the tail end of the arrow, you'll see a little notch, or nock as we call it. What you do first is attach this notch to the bowstring, like this."

Urjah did as he said, sliding the arrow's notched rear onto the bow's string so that its front half rested against the limb of wood. "Now, you pull onto the string, drawing the arrow back with it, while you aim its point at your target like you would a spear," he said slowly, his instructions clear. "The further back you pull, the further the arrow will fly and the harder it will hit."

He acted out his own instructions, aiming his arrow at the trunk of a fan palm which slanted over the river's shore a couple of paces away. When he let go of the bowstring, the arrow zipped into the tree with a hard thunk.

Oja gasped. "So it's a way to throw a spear further than you can with your arm?"

"Yes, that's it. Though the arrow won't pack as much of a punch as the big spears you're used to. It's better for smaller prey than larger ones, unless you apply poison to the tip. Now, you try."

Urjah handed the bow and quiver to Oja. She fumbled a bit trying to nock the arrow onto the bowstring and then drawing it back against the wood. Both bow and arrow wobbled in her grip as she tried to aim at the palm tree.

"You need to hold it steady," Urjah said.

With his hand, he nudged the bow to stand in an upright position in Oja's hand. She tensed her arm muscles to keep it still, holding her breath as she did when about to throw a spear.

"Now, let go."

Her fingers parted as he advised. The arrow flew from the bow and hit a short distance above Urjah's on the palm tree.

Urjah patted Oja on the shoulder. "Not bad! Why don't you practice some more on those waterbuck over there—"

She looked over. The waterbuck herd had vanished. The reason became clear. A deep rumbling sound, coupled with heavy squishing into the mud of the riverbank and the cracking of branches, suggested what spooked them.

Out from the tree shadows lumbered the most colossal elephant Oja had ever seen. Tusks longer than the height of most men swept down to the ground from its scarred face, an obsidian spearhead embedded into the base of the right tusk. More broken spears and arrows studded its wrinkled dust-yellowed hide, with the flesh around some swollen into hideous callus-like bumps. As the savanna giant approached Oja and Urjah, it flared out its broad, fan-like ears while swaying its head sideways, its rumble a threatening growl.

Urjah's complexion became paler than normal. "That's Old Wounded," he whispered from the corner of his mouth. "He's the one who killed my mother and father."

"I can see why he would attack people like that," Oja said. "Look at the poor thing!"

The elephant grumbled louder while brandishing his tusks with greater fervor. The way he swung his foreleg back and forth over the earth reminded Oja of the rhinoceros.

"We should run," she said.

"No," Urjah replied. "We'll stand our ground. Show him we won't let him bully us away."

Old Wounded stomped his other foreleg into the earth with a frustrated harrumph. Oja moved one leg backward, but Urjah clenched his hand hard on her shoulder and pulled her closer to himself.

"I really do think he wants us to leave," Oja said.

Urjah smirked at her. "Then we'll make him leave instead."

He bared his teeth while taunting the elephant with hollers and hoots, beating his chest like one of the giant apes said to live in the jungles beyond the western ranges. Again the elephant pounded his front legs on the soil, thrashing his trunk and tusks more violently than before. Then Urjah did what even she at her boldest would not have dared: he swiped the bow from her hands, together with an arrow from the quiver, and shot Old Wounded in the forehead.

With a blaring trumpet that drowned out all other sounds in the world, the titan stormed toward Urjah. Every thunderous step of Old Wounded's feet shook the earth underneath. He thrust his trunk onto the young man, coiled it around his neck, and hurled him into the trunk of a nearby wattle tree. Blood smeared down from the point of collision as the boy rolled down to the tree's roots. Walking over to where Urjah lay and then prodding his body with one foreleg, the elephant curled the tip of his trunk into a fist-like club and raised it high over his victim, ready to deliver one final blow.

Oja snatched the bow her friend had dropped and shot the elephant in the rear end.

Turning away from the fallen Urjah, the beast began to charge her. She dashed into the woods, zigzagging between the trees to throw her pursuer off her path. But the behemoth was able to keep up with her by simply crashing his ten-ton bulk straight through the vegetation. It was not long before the elephant was on her heels, his trumpeting nearly loud enough to shatter her eardrums.

With a swing of his trunk, Old Wounded swatted Oja off her feet. She landed onto a bush with thorns that pricked and clawed at her skin, drawing blood. If the elephant caught her as she struggled to free herself of the plant's spiky clutches, he would surely crush her.

Wait . . . if the monster wanted her dead, maybe she should give it what he wanted.

She stopped all movement. Even the rise and fall of her breathing. Her limbs fell limp as her head rolled aside, staring into space as if no life remained in them. She held her breath while caving in her stomach to disguise its natural rising and sinking. As the elephant stood over her and stroked her body with his trunk, she suppressed any impulse to move a muscle or breathe.

Sensing his kill complete, Old Wounded lumbered away into the woods, leaving her. Only after he disappeared into the tree shadows did Oja tear herself out of the thornbush, careful not to yelp in pain. Once free, she wiped perspiration off her brow and sighed deeply, relieved to still be alive. She would need many bandages to cover all the scratches on her body.

As for Urjah . . . was he alright as well?

CHAPTER SEVEN
Urjah Wounded

Oja followed the path of trampled undergrowth and splintered trees the elephant had left as it pursued her. She found Urjah still sprawled over the roots of the wattle tree, where she had left him. Red fluid drenched half of his face, with more flowing out of his nostrils. A shard of bone stuck out of the side of the young man's skull.

From the branches above, a vulture squawked. More of the bald-headed birds were flocking over to perch, the same opportunistic glints in their eyes. They sensed what Oja dreaded more than anything else.

She knelt over Urjah to cradle his head in her arms. "Tell me you'll make it."

"I don't . . . know about that, Oja." His voice was reduced to a coughing croak. "But even if I don't . . . I won't mind. It—it'll mean that . . . I will see my mother and father again . . . soon."

"No! You can't leave like this. Not when you're still so young."

"Do not worry . . . about me. Take my bow and my spear with you. If you still . . . long for company . . . go down the river . . . and find the village of my mother and father . . ."

Urjah's breathing grew more shallow until it broke up and changed into a gagging rattle. Then silence. The last movement of his body was the closing of his eyes, falling into a deep, eternal slumber. A slumber where he would dream himself into the domain of the ancestors, alongside the man and woman who raised him by themselves until they too passed.

Oja had only known Urjah for one night and one morning. Yet this loss wounded her heart as much as if she had lost a member of her family. Tears dripped from her face onto his, washing clean white streaks through his blood. Under her breath, she murmured for the ancestors to accept his soul among them.

Admittedly, Urjah's own foolishness had brought Old Wounded's wrath upon him. Yet somehow Oja could not help but wonder if he had confronted the beast to impress her. If she had never come into his territory, and built the campfire near his dwelling, he might have lived to see past his twentieth rainy season. *Was this my fault?* She wondered. *Just like being separated from my people right now is my fault?*

No, Oja, she thought through her tears, *don't blame yourself for his loss. He made his own choice. Enough with this pitying and blaming yourself!*

A white-backed vulture's hooked beak scratched Oja on the shoulder. The entire flock had already descended to form a tight circle around her and Urjah. They closed in with impatient cawing. Oja swiped the bow at the birds to drive them back, hissing and baring her teeth at them. They retorted by flapping their wings furiously while jabbing their beaks at her like spears. Their attacks added to her wounds little by little.

There was no point in resisting them any further. Oja fled straight through the flock until they were behind her, leaving them to pounce on Urjah's body. She pressed her hands over her ears to block out the noise of them tearing through flesh and bone, squabbling among themselves for the choicest cuts of human flesh. To hear a human body being reduced to scraps drenched with blood and drool squeezed her stomach with nausea. Especially of a young man she'd already begun caring about.

The vultures withdrew from their meal to flutter away into the heavens, quicker than she expected. She walked back to Urjah's body. All that remained was a disarticulated skeleton with tiny slivers of flesh still clinging to the bones. It would not be long before even these attracted other scavengers such as jackals and striped hyenas, whose jaws could crack open those bones the vultures couldn't. Oja could not allow that to happen. The boy's remains were desecrated enough as it was.

She scooped up as many of Urjah's bones as she could in her arms, the skull first among them. Even cleansed of its flesh and organs, the skeleton was a burdensome load to bear as she walked through the woodland back to the hut they had shared the previous night. Laying his bones in a pile within the hut, she took Urjah's fishing spear and pierced the floor with it, excavating as much earth as its bone point could support. The weapon was far from the ideal digging stick, but she had nothing else better around her.

Morning gave way to midday, and then to late day until she excavated a hole sufficiently big. Placing the bones that had been Urjah in it, she knelt over it and shut her eyes, beginning her invocation:

"O ancestors upon ancestors, please accept young Urjah among yourselves. He was born into a hard life, with a curse on his skin and only his mother and father to raise him up. I, Oja, only knew him for a night and a morning, yet I know that he deserved better than what he got. Please, I implore you, take him in. See that he has a better life in the next world than he had in ours. And may he watch over us as you watched over him."

After a moment of silence, she dumped the dirt back into the hole to cover what had once been Urjah, smearing it over to disguise the hole as much as she could. She'd given him the honorable burial he was due.

She was alone again. By now, her people must have noticed her disappearance. They must have taken her for dead, perhaps honoring her passing with a somber ritual of their own. They would not have her body to bury, of course, but they would still sing together in her honor, praying for the ancestors to take her in too. And all because her foolishness had separated her from them, much as Urjah's foolishness had cost him his life.

There could be no turning back now. Before his passing to the next life, Urjah told Oja to go down the river and find the village of his family. There, she would no longer be by herself. There, she would have a new band to call her own.

She wiped the dirt off the spear and slung it over her back underneath the quiver's strap. With her cheeks still damp from her mourning tears, she left the hut and Urjah's buried body behind and walked into the wilderness.

CHAPTER EIGHT
The Men in the Floating Log

Thrice the sun drifted on its arcing path over the earth. Oja kept close to the river throughout as she trekked parallel to its course. Not only did it give her water and direction for her journey, but she knew that it could provide food as well.

She didn't use Urjah's spear for fishing the way he had, since she never had experience with that skill. Her people always caught their prey on land rather than in water. Instead, she focused on the animals that hung around the river's edge, or went down there to drink. They would provide her with meat. Once she caught a large turtle wading among the reeds. Prying open the reptile's shell with the spear took exhaustive effort, but once accomplished, its meat would keep her sated for the next couple of days. And its carapace allowed her to scoop up greater quantities of water than her cupped hands alone.

Nonetheless, the river was not only a place of bounty. Whenever Oja spotted crocodiles or hippopotamuses, she retreated into the woods until they had swum or wallowed past. On other occasions, predators of the plains and forest ventured down to the river, either for drink or to prey on thirsty herbivores. She hid from them by climbing into trees or crouching behind rocks, always clutching her spear.

She favored the spear, whether procuring food or protecting herself. It was more familiar to her than the bow and arrow, and she did not want to risk emptying her quiver of arrows with missed shots before she became proficient. Maybe, after finding the village, she would practice using her new weapon more.

Early on the fourth day, the sun began creeping up from the woodland treetops. She stumbled upon a rectangular pillar of rock standing as tall as a human being on the riverbank.

Oja's first impulse was to regard it as yet another natural out-cropping. There were plenty in this area. A second look revealed a curious impression on the side of the rock shaped exactly like a lizard, complete with a head, sprawling limbs and five-clawed hands, and a curved tail. Glistening within this image were spots and bands of a reflective yellow paint that matched the patterns of what she knew as a river monitor. It was rather like the images her people would paint on boulders and inside caves during sacred occasions, such as welcoming the arrival of the annual rains, except this one seemed to have been chiseled into the rock before the paint was applied.

Was this depiction of a monitor the work of the people whose village lay ahead? Or some other people? Whoever they were, why would they leave such an image behind in the first place? It must have taken them hours to carve it into the rock, she guessed.

And what was that glossy yellow substance used for the paint? Oja brushed her fingertips over it and rubbed them together. The substance flecked off in little sparkling specks. It was nothing like anything she had ever seen before.

Someone whistled and then called out to her. "You there! Who are you, and what are you doing here?"

She followed the voice and saw two men on the river, both seated within a hollowed-out floating log. The one in the back held a long stick with a flattened tip, while the man in front clutched a fishing spear not unlike the one Urjah had given to her. But these men were of the same black complexion as Oja and the rest of humankind.

"Where am I?" Oja shouted back.

The man with the spear pointed his free hand to the column of rock with the lizard image she had been puzzling over. "That marks the edge of our land, the land of the Monitor Village. You were about to trespass onto our land, weren't you?"

"She doesn't know that, Bukti," the man with the flat-tipped stick said. He directed his gaze to Oja. "You're not from around here, are you?"

"I'm from the plains atop the high cliffs to the north. Could you come over here? I don't want to wear my voice out by yelling at you like this!"

The man at the back of the hollowed log stroked the water's surface with his modified stick, propelling it across the river until its front tip ground over the mud on the riverbank. As the men hopped out to approach Oja, she noticed that their ostrich egg-shell–bead necklaces had ovular centerpieces crafted from the same yellow lustrous substance as the monitor lizard engraving. Wrapped around their hips were skirts woven from reeds or grass like baskets, instead of the hide loincloths Oja and her people wore.

The man called Bukti squinted. "Why is a woman like you carrying the weapons of men? You have both a spear and a bow!"

"It was a young man named Urjah—may his ancestors watch over him—who gave them to me," Oja said. "And I am a woman of the plains. Among my people, both men and women may carry whatever weapons they please."

"A woman of the plains, you say?" the second man said. "What would one of your kind be doing here by yourself along the river?"

Oja gazed toward the north, biting her lip. "It is a long story, but it should be enough to say that . . . fate made me fall into this place. Call me Oja. Who are you, and what were you doing out on that log?"

"You mean our canoe?" Bukti tapped the front of the hollowed log. "We were searching for new fishing grounds. I am Bukti, and this would be my little brother, Roggan. So, Oja, since you've 'fallen down' here, where do you plan to go next?"

"Urjah told me that the village of his parents lay downriver of here. I presume that would be your village as well?"

"So you want to become one of the Monitor people, woman from the plains?" Roggan asked. "As much as we would like to welcome you in, do you know the ways of the river people are different from yours?"

"I know that all too well, but everyone must have people to live among. I will learn your ways if you accept me as one of your own."

Bukti and Roggan looked at one another and shrugged.

"If so, you can come with us in our canoe," Bukti said.

When the two men returned to their canoe, they opened more space between them so Oja could nestle in. The vessel wobbled sideways as she took her seat within the cavity dug out of the wood.

"Are you sure this thing is sturdy enough to carry the three of us?" she asked.

"It carries more than three all the time," Bukti assured her with a smile. "If anything, you'll be lighter than most loads it can carry."

"I do have one thing to ask you, though," Roggan said. "Could you row with your spear like it was an oar?"

Oja blinked at him. "What's an oar?"

Roggan held up his stick with the wide flattened tip. "You use it to 'row'—to stroke the water so that you move the canoe across it."

"Oh, like you were doing a moment ago? Sure, I can try!"

She inserted her spear's point through the water's surface and tried to "row" in imitation of what she had seen Roggan do. To her amazement, her motion pushed the canoe off the bank toward the middle of the river. Both Roggan and Bukti hooted in praise.

"Not bad at all—especially for a woman," Roggan said. "Now, you row from the left side, while I row from the right. That will keep our path going down the river straight."

"Before we head back home, though, we need fish," Bukti added. He pushed toward Oja a lidded basket that had been sitting between them. "How about you be the one to give the fish the bait?"

Oja took off the basket's lid, and the stink of decaying flesh flowed out like a torrent of acrid smoke. Fanning the odor away from her nose, she pierced one of the scraps of meat with her spear's tip and dipped it back into the river. Blood flowed out of the piece of bait, creating a cloud within the water.

They waited beneath the passing sun until a plump catfish swam into view. It bit onto the bait, tugging onto Oja's spear with surprising force until Bukti stabbed it in the flank. He whispered his gratitude to the fish as he hauled it into the canoe. The catfish, which was as long and thick as his arm, landed next to the basket of bait.

"That should feed us for a few days," he said.

Roggan snickered. "With your appetite, brother, I don't know if it'll last that long."

Oja had not known Bukti long enough to laugh at his brother's barb, but she could understand the meaning of the joke. Bukti was the taller and more muscular of the pair, so he would need more meat to feed him, and Oja did not find him unattractive, either. She would sooner let a man with his physique gaze at her with desire than she would Tukar, back within her band.

Something erupted from the water next to Roggan. He screamed as he fell out of the canoe, the resulting splash rocking the vessel almost to the point of capsizing.

A crocodile had snatched him by his arm!

He hollered in desperate agony as the giant reptile thrashed him about in its wedge-shaped jaws, staining the water crimson with more blood. Calling out for his brother, Bukti threw his spear at the monster, but it merely bounced off the thick scaly armor of the saurian predator's back.

Oja pulled out her knife and dove into the river. She kicked hard to propel herself forward until she reached the crocodile and wrung her arm around its neck. She hammered her knife at where she thought its jugular would be. The beast shook itself with even greater intensity until it forced her to release her grip. It let go of the wounded Roggan and sped after her with jaws agape, its swishing tail propelling it through the murky depths at a superhuman velocity.

As she sank toward the river bottom, Oja spotted the gleam from the point of Bukti's fallen spear below her. She dove again, dodging the crocodile's next attack by a narrow breadth, and snatched the weapon out of the aquatic undergrowth. Once she had armed herself, she thrust the spear into the reptile's exposed breast above her. Blood billowed. The crocodile, now dying from the mortal wound, descended to the bottom, attracting schools of scavenging fish the way a dying animal on land would draw in vultures.

She retrieved Bukti's spear from the crocodile and launched back to the surface, gulping in a great breath of air. She found Roggan back on the canoe with his brother, panting and wincing in pain. Bukti must have pulled him up from the water, and both of the men were staring at her with eyes wide open.

"Did you . . . kill that crocodile yourself?" Bukti asked as he reached out his arms to lift Oja into the canoe.

Oja nodded as she spewed out a mouthful of river water. "It was a vicious fight, but yes, I did. Don't think I was bad at it, either—for a woman."

"Sorry . . . about that . . ." Roggan said, groaning as he rubbed the wounds on his mangled arm. "That was impressive . . . for anyone."

A red blob floated to the river's surface and spread out, marking where the crocodile had fallen. That was the first time in a long while Oja had killed anything bigger than a turtle. If Uru and Namak, or anyone else from her old band, would have witnessed her in action, they would dance and chant her name in song the entire night. And when the people of the Monitor Village find out about what she had just done on Roggan's behalf, they would have to let her in among them without any quarrel.

Oja beamed with pride, like a lion who had brought down its prey.

CHAPTER NINE
Uru's Vision

Uru found herself in a field of grass as high as her waist, each of its orange blades as thick as the point of the spear she held in her hand. Overhead swirled black smoke-like clouds in a scarlet sky, the sun bleeding rays of yellow light through them. In all directions, the flat orange grassland sprawled to eternity, with neither rock nor tree in sight to break up the rolling monotony. Nor could Uru make out any hills or mountains from beyond the horizon like she could on the plains she and her people had always roamed.

Yet, wherever in the world she was, she was not alone.

A short distance away, a herd of blue kudu grazed, yellow stripes running down their flanks. The bulls of the herd sported metallic horns that twisted twice as tall as those of normal kudu. All appeared engrossed in their feeding, not even one raising its head to survey for danger the way a typical antelope would.

Uru licked her lips. If she was to be stuck in this alien world without any company other than these kudu, she might as well feed herself.

She flung her spear at the nearest kudu. The missile should have hit the animal in the flank, but instead it passed through as if the kudu were a mere apparition. Nonetheless, it bleated in shock, and then the whole herd bolted away until they disappeared into the air.

Uru walked over to where her spear should have landed. She did not find it. She ran her hand through the grass, exposing indigo soil underneath, yet it did not turn up. It must have vanished like the kudu.

Once she rose back to her feet, she found Oja standing right in front of her. "Why have you forsaken me?" she asked, her voice an echo.

"I have not forsaken you," Uru said. "You fell into the rapids, didn't you?"

"That does not mean I am dead," Oja said. "You and Namak have given up on me. Why?"

And then she was gone. Along with the spear and the kudu.

The black clouds above expanded into one another until they formed one thick, unbroken layer with neither sky nor sun showing through. From them descended purple droplets of water, increasing until they grew into a rainstorm. Red lightning streaked across the sky, and thunder cracked as the violet water rose up to Uru's ankles, her knees, and above her waist, submerging the entire field. It kept on rising until Uru found herself being tossed around in a turbulent ocean stirred up by a howling wind.

She flailed her arms in a struggle to keep her head above the raging sea's surface, but it pulled her into its depths like an invisible octopus dragging her down with its tentacles. Around her swam schools of glossy black fish, converging into a crowd, gawking all around her. She looked into Oja's face on all of them.

"Why have you forsaken me?" they said in reverberant unison, their voices Oja's. "Why have you given up on me . . ."

They chanted those two lines over and over as Uru sank further into the black abyss. Even after it had become too dark to see anything, their voices still resounded.

And then Uru woke up.

Only late in the morning did Uru finally force herself out of her shelter, carrying her spear. She still kept rubbing her eyelids as she walked through the camp to a circle of rocks near the waterhole where she and the other young women of the band spent their idle time. Namak was already there, braiding the hair of her younger sister, Iyi, while they gossiped together.

"The bags under your eyes are even darker than before," Namak said. "You've had trouble sleeping, haven't you?"

Uru picked up a little fragment of stone and started chipping it against her spear's point to keep it sharp. "I had another one of those dreams. I don't understand. They all seem to be the same dream, over and over again."

"What happens in them?"

"I keep seeing Oja again. She's always telling me I have forsaken her, that I've turned my back on her somehow."

"Maybe it's a sign that she's still alive?" Iyi asked.

"That's what I believe too. And as long as she's out there, wherever she is, she'll haunt my dreams forever."

"So what are you suggesting?" Namak asked. "Oja could very well be alive, but going down those rapids would have taken her to another part of the world, cut off from us. What do you want us to do, climb down those southern cliffs and hope she's waiting there at the bottom?"

"The cliffs may not go on forever. For all you and I know, the land might slope down somewhere so that we could simply hike down to wherever she is. But even if it doesn't, we shouldn't give up on her yet. Not when she's telling me that she's out there in my dreams every night."

Namak paused to gaze at the horizon to the south. "You know what, Uru, I've been thinking of Oja a lot too. Life isn't the same without her. Curse my ancestors, I shouldn't have told her that you and I would never hunt with her again. Why else would she go missing in the first place?"

"So, you'll help me look for her again?"

"How long would it take? How far would she have gone by now? Even if we do find her, the rest of the band would have moved on and we would be lost by ourselves forever."

"Not if the people agreed to wait for us here. Come to think of it, your grandfather has seen many different places in his long life. Might he know what lies to the south?"

Namak shrugged. "It's worth a try . . . if you could get him to wake up."

Iyi burst into a girlish giggle. "Good luck on that! Wait, can I come with you on your journey?"

"Sorry, little sister, you're needed with the band," Namak said. "You could give Lu and Tukar company on their hunts."

"Ugh, those two . . ." Iyi's face scrunched into an ugly grimace as she stuck out her tongue. "I'd sooner hunt with a pack of filthy jackals!"

"Then you can dig up tubers with the elders," Uru said. "Or look for another hunting partner if you must. The point is, you are too young to go with us. You could get hurt. Or killed."

"And I don't want to lose you like we did Oja," Namak added.

Iyi pouted her lip, then nodded. "I understand."

"Good. You do not know how much you mean to me and our family."

While Namak continued braiding her sister's hair, Uru headed to the middle of the encampment where all the elders slept, protected on all sides by younger, stronger members of the band. Most of the elders appeared to be away already, carrying out their chores or chatting with one another elsewhere. Nonetheless, a loud snore growled from one of the innermost shelters. Following the source of the noise, Uru found Namak and Iyi's grandfather, Kulro, curled up inside, his bony frame wrapped within a ragged sheet of zebra hide.

Uru said his name twice, both times receiving no response from the dozing old man. Her next resort was to gently rub him on the shoulder.

Kulro exploded into a frenzy of swinging fists and legs as he rolled onto his back. "Cursed ancestors, can't you let a man of many rains get his rest?"

"Calm down, old one," Uru said. "I need your wisdom."

"Oh, wisdom, you say, young Uru? If it's my wisdom you seek, I'll be happy to share it. Never has anyone sought me out for that, out of all the elders in the band."

"I thought a man as well-traveled as you would know better than most. So what do you know of the land to the south? I know there are cliffs that go down there, and I believe my friend Oja lies beyond their bottom. I have visions of her every night."

Kulro grinned, exposing his weathered teeth. "Good for you that I know something about the south, then. They say a great river flows through the land beyond the bottom of the cliffs, and that there are many big camps set up alongside its course. If one were to scale down the cliffs, they might find Oja in one of those camps. You're not planning to track her down yourself, are you?"

"In truth, I am, and I plan to take Namak along with me. Could you talk the band into staying right here by the waterhole while we are gone?"

"Oh, I don't know about that. Depending on how long you're gone, we might eat up all the food around here before you two come back with Oja."

"Maybe not. Even if we are gone for more than a few days, the rains cannot be too far off now. Doubtless they will bring forth plenty of berries and fruit to feed the people in the meantime."

Kulro scratched his dusty hair. "I can only hope you are proved right, Uru. I will try to talk the band into staying here when we go to tonight's campfire. I warn you, though, I do not foresee persuading them with ease."

"Do what you can. Your granddaughter and I will argue our case as well."

"In case you cannot get the band to agree, though, what do you plan on doing, young one?"

That was a good question. Uru did not want to sneak out without her people knowing, or else they would consider her and Namak as lost as Oja. But how else could she quell the visions that haunted her sleep every night? If she were to ignore them, then she truly would be forsaking Oja.

"I do not know," she told Kulro. "All I know is that Oja is out there, somewhere. And she is waiting for us."

CHAPTER TEN
The Village

Twice again the sun and the moon chased one another across the sky since Oja met the two men in the floating log, the canoe. She and Bukti spent the majority of both days rowing down the river, ignoring the burning soreness of their forelimbs as much as they could, while Roggan rested at the back with mud from the riverbank smeared over his wounds to block out any malicious spirits that could sicken him even more.

Three times each day, they paused from rowing to harpoon more fish, and each night, they rowed to the bank to make camp. All other hours were spent churning the water with their oars, a labor every bit as monotonous as it was exhausting.

Late in the third day, after the three had rounded another bend in the river, they spotted a tall structure standing on a rocky islet jutting up from the middle of the river. The structure looked much the same as Urjah's old hut at its top, albeit with a long and narrow opening cut into its side. It perched on four wooden stilts as high as giraffes were tall, with a ladder of rope and wooden planks hanging down from the back. As the canoe drew nearer to this bizarre building, Oja spotted a face and pair of human eyes looking out from an opening in the wall.

"Who goes there?" a youthful male voice shouted from atop the tower.

"It is us, Bukti and Roggan," Bukti called back. "And we bring with us a newcomer, a woman named Oja."

The face of a boy no older than fifteen rains popped out from the tower's window. His eyes seemed to sparkle even from a distance as they fell upon Oja.

"Oh, you mean her?" he said. "She wouldn't have become your woman, would she, Bukti?"

Bukti chuckled. "Not yet, little Dako, not yet." He turned to Oja with a teasing smirk. "I see our sentry has already taken a liking to you."

Oja shook her head and rolled her eyes. "You men are all the same."

"Don't act like you women are any better," Roggan said. "I've seen the way you look at Bukti."

That prompted Bukti to rub his hand over his hair while giving Oja a mischievous wink.

She grumbled in resignation. "Fair enough."

"Anyway, I wouldn't worry about young Dako if I were you, Oja," Bukti said. "He wouldn't hurt a dung beetle, much less a woman. He's simply going through that phase of life all boys—and girls—go through. But he still needs to grow more before he can have what he wants, if you know what I mean."

"I heard that!" Dako cried out from the tower again. "So why is the woman coming in with you? She looks the way one of those women of the plains are said to look."

"That is true," Oja responded. "I became separated from my own people through an accident, and I don't think I will ever see them again. I wish to become one among your people."

Dako squinted at her, blinking. "You . . . wish to become one of us? Whoa, it's not often you see those of the plains who want to settle down among us river people. You really want to do that, woman?"

"Where else can I find human companionship in this land? Unless I were to meet other people of the plains around here, I see no other choice but to join your people."

"Alright, you can speak to our chieftain about that. But I warn you, becoming one of the Monitor people will not be easy. She must approve of you. You may pass."

As Oja and Bukti rowed the canoe past the tower, she spied Dako still gazing down at her from its back entryway with boyish longing. Were there no girls his age in the village that he could court? If so, she would pity him. But on the other hand, the young man would need to learn sooner or later that simply desiring a woman did not mean he could have his way without her consent.

And who was this woman "chieftain" the sentry had spoken of? Why did Oja need her approval to join the village? Considering everything else she had learned about women's places among the river people, everything they do falling behind a man, it did not make sense that a woman would hold that kind of influence among them.

But Dako may have raised a good point. Maybe there was a reason most people of the plains did not abandon their way of life to live among these strange river people. But where else could she live in this land below the cliffs?

An islet of rock rose behind the one supporting the sentry's tower. It supported a stout, pillar-like monolith, the same image of a monitor lizard inscribed into it as the one she had seen the day she met Bukti and Roggan. It even sported the same stripes and spots of glossy yellow paint.

Bukti nodded his head as they passed the monolith. "Welcome to the village of the Monitor people!"

The first thing Oja spotted beyond the inscribed rock was a fence of wooden stakes, each as tall as a human. It ran along the far edge of the northern bank, continuing past the next bend in the river. From behind the fence rose several dozen conical thatched roofs packed closely together, indicating a much greater number of dwellings than she had ever seen in one camp. Among these structures rose many columns of smoke, presumably from their cooking fires, the columns merging into a layer of pale gray smog that floated between the village and the heavens. Even from the canoe, Oja could catch a faint whiff of the smoke.

She saw an opening in the fence framed by an arching pair of elephant tusks bound together with twine at the tips, a monitor lizard's skull dangling from the point of binding. Several other dugout canoes rested on the riverbank's edge in front of the entryway. Bukti and Oja rowed to that point and dragged it ashore after helping the recovering Roggan out of the canoe and to his feet.

A small group of people rushed through the village entrance to encircle them. All wore the same woven-reed skirts as Bukti and Roggan, along with pendants of that shiny yellow rock attached to their necklaces. One, a balding man who looked to have seen many rains, embraced Bukti and Roggan together in his skinny arms.

"My sons have returned!" he announced. "What happened to you, Roggan? You've mud all over your arm!"

"I had a little confrontation with a crocodile out on the river, Father," Roggan said. "I owe my survival to this brave young woman, Oja, who killed it all by herself. Oja, meet our father, Pok."

Soft warmth blushed in Oja's cheeks. "It wasn't that hard, really."

The villagers' eyes fell upon her without blinking. The old man Pok rubbed his pate with his hand. "You're . . . not from any of the river villages, are you?" he asked.

"I come from the plains above the cliffs to the far north," Oja said. "But I found myself stranded in these lands, and since I cannot return to my people, I seek to become one of you. Where is your chieftain?"

Pok turned his head to gaze at the tusked entrance. "You mean my daughter? I can take you to her. But be warned, she does not tend to trust strangers who have come here unexpectedly."

"Why not?"

"I don't blame her, really. It is her duty to keep our people as safe as she can. Come, let us hope you are able to make her warm up to you."

Oja followed the man through the opening beneath the arching tusks. A broad street of trampled earth cut straight through the village, dividing it in half. From the sides of this avenue branched thinner, winding paths which led to clusters of huts that made up the bulk of the settlement. The sheer amount of homes along the road, each larger than the temporary shelters her people built to sleep in, overwhelmed Oja's mind. It was awe-inspiring. There must have been as many families calling this community home as there were termites swarming within one of the big mounds on the savanna.

All of the people gawked at her as she passed them. Children put down their clay-figurine toys to point at Oja while asking their nearest elders about the strange visitor in skimpy animal-hide clothes. The adults, having no answer, would pull them away from her sight as if to protect them from a predator. Otherwise, the looks appeared more like wide-eyed stupefaction than hostile glares. They didn't distrust her outright, but they couldn't believe a person like her would be walking past them, either.

Still, it made Oja shudder to be the center of so much attention from the Monitor people. Or maybe that was her reaction to the odors of smog and fish from the river, drying on racks that hung over the place.

"Don't mind them so much," Pok said. "Once we put some proper clothes on you, you'll fit right in like one of us."

Oja huffed at the phrase "proper clothes." But this was not the time to quarrel with her host.

They reached a point where the main street started to ascend the slope of a stout hillock or mound, running through another elephant-tusk archway at the base. Once they hiked up the path to the summit, Oja trained her eyes on the entire sprawl of the village around them, the river bordering it to the south and an expanse of plains stretching to its north. Huts that had impressed her with their size only moments earlier now seemed almost as puny as ant-hills from this elevated vantage, with the people becoming small as scurrying ants.

Something fuzzy rubbed Oja's calves. She looked down to see a wildcat pacing around her legs, an ivory collar girdling its neck. Pok scooped it up in his arms with gentle care and stroked its head with an affectionate chuckle.

"I see you've met our little Yowh," he said. "I think he's already taken a liking to you."

"You . . . keep cats around?" Oja asked. "Aren't you worried about them stealing your meat?"

"Not at all. They keep the rats away, and they're always good company."

They stepped onto a circular dirt plaza ringed by tall, slender megaliths, each with reliefs of a crawling monitor lizard carved into it. Along the plaza's opposite side stood a hut twice as big as any other Oja had seen in the village so far, with another pair of tusks framing its entryway. The entire hut was built of elephant bones that had been lashed together, rather than sticks, like the other huts.

When he approached this edifice of bone and thatch, Pok rested on one knee and whistled. "O Chieftain, I beg you to come forth. You have a visitor who requests your judgment!"

Out strutted a woman who looked to be a few rains older than Oja, a mantle of leopard skin draped around one shoulder and several rings of lion fangs and beads of the shiny yellow substance looped around her neck. A headdress of ostrich and fishing-eagle feathers swayed over her face as she regarded Oja with half-shut eyes, head tilted back. Her fingers squeezed onto an ebony staff with a monitor lizard's skull glued to its top with tar.

"Who are you who has come for my judgment?" the chieftain asked Oja, almost like an announcement.

Oja realized that Pok was prostrating himself before his own daughter.

"Excuse me, am I supposed to be lying down like him?" Oja asked.

"I see you are new to these lands, then," the chieftain said. "I am Nyzai, chieftain of the Monitor Village. And, as such, I do demand the respect you owe me."

Oja knelt at Nyzai's feet, imitating Pok, recognizing the supreme respect the woman received.

"That shall suffice. So who are you, newcomer, and why do you come to our village?"

"You may call me Oja. I come not from the lands along the river, but from the plains atop the cliffs to the north. I've found myself separated from my people, and so I wish to join the Monitor people as one of them. Will you allow me this, as my chieftain?"

Nyzai placed her chin on the flat of her hand while squinting at Oja. "Well, I can't say I've ever had an outsider, let alone one of the open plains, simply come into my village asking to become one of my people. I find that very strange. Do you even know any of our customs, woman of the plains?"

"I . . . spent a brief amount of time with a young man whose parents came from your village. His name was Urjah, and I learned a few things about the river people through him."

"Urjah? Where have I heard that name before . . . wait, he was the one born cursed with whiteness that my mother told me about when I was a girl! How long have you been learning these 'few things' with him?"

Oja lowered her head in regret. "Sadly, only one night and one morning. A rogue elephant killed him out in the bush. But you must trust me, O Chieftain, I can learn all your ways if you give me the chance to live among you."

Pok nodded. "Not to mention, she has already saved our Roggan from a crocodile out on the river before coming here. I believe, my daughter, that you owe her your gratitude."

The chieftain widened her eyes at Oja, who crossed her arms with a proud grin.

"You . . . saved my brother . . . from a crocodile?" Nyzai stammered.

"And slew it all by myself, too," Oja said. "With a knife and spear."

"You lie!"

Pok shook his head. "Roggan told me so himself after he and Bukti brought her here."

The chieftain's eyes switched between her father and Oja before she sighed with resignation. "If that is so . . . then, Oja, you must not be like any other women in the world, not even me," she said.

"Maybe not you women of the villages, but we women of the plains are not like you," Oja replied.

"Well . . . then I do owe you my thanks. Without you, my little brother would have perished. Still, since you are a woman of the plains, having someone like you among us would be like trying to tame a leopard once it is old. You would be too used to your old ways to change for us."

"With all due respect, O Chieftain, this Oja is no old leopard," Pok interjected. "Why, she appears even younger than yourself! I see no reason why she cannot learn to fit into our culture. Please, I implore you, give her a chance."

"And, if you do not let me in, then where else can I go?" Oja added. "I would be out in the wild all alone, forced to fend for myself, until the day I pass on to my ancestors. You do not wish for anyone to suffer that fate, do you?"

Nyzai sighed, the hardness of her expression melting into a hint of pity. "No, I do not wish suffering upon anyone. Still, I cannot let any outsider simply walk into my village and claim herself as one of my people, not even one who has risked her life for my kin. You will have to earn your way in."

"Earn my way in? What do you mean?"

The chieftain tapped a yellow bead on one of her several necklaces. "You know what this is? This is gold, the stone borne from the sun. We dig it up from the valley to the north of here. What you must do, Oja, is obtain a nugget of your own."

Oja raised an eyebrow. "I am willing to do that, Chieftain. That doesn't sound so hard."

"It wouldn't be, except that valley is where several clans of the ape-people live," Pok said. "And, as you should know already, their kind doesn't like humans that much."

"But ape-people aren't as clever as we are," Oja said. "They don't even know how to make fire. I do not see any problem at all."

"I admire your courage and your confidence," Nyzai said. "But, just to be safe, I will not have you go there by yourself. I shall have my brother Bukti accompany you."

"Why do you believe I need him, if I can ask? I've been out there by myself for enough days now. Like I said, I can handle a few ape-people. I handled that crocodile, didn't I?"

"Ape-people hunt in troops, and a troop of them could be more trouble than one crocodile. So, whether you accept it or not, Bukti will go with you to the valley. And that is final!" Nyzai pounded the ground with her scepter to emphasize her point.

Oja grumbled with a shrug. "Alright, so when should we leave for this valley?"

The chieftain nodded to Pok. "Tomorrow. My father here shall take you in for the night. Do sleep well, Oja, for you will need it."

CHAPTER ELEVEN
Debate at the Waterhole

There was no meat roasting over the campfire as night cast its star-dusted shadow over the land. It was not for a lack of effort on the hunters' part. Far from it, for Uru and Namak had worn their feet out and drenched themselves in perspiration after spending the entire day combing the savanna around the waterhole for wild game. And they had found not even the smallest edible creature, except a locust Namak had plucked from a blade of grass a little before sundown. It served as no more than a crispy snack with barely enough moisture to wash the mouth of dryness, barely smoothing down the edge of her hunger.

The big talk had yet to begin. Already Namak was unsure of the position she and Uru, together with old Kulro, were going to argue for.

Across the fire from where they sat, Lu gnawed on a hare bone like a hyena that was thirsty for its marrow. He and his friend Tukar had also reported finding no meat around the waterhole. Even if that had not been the case, however, Namak could count on him to oppose any proposition she or Uru put forward. The boy hadn't exactly acted like his own sister's departure affected him that much the past several days.

Sure enough, he established his position before either of the huntresses had even spoken. "We ought to move away from this waterhole before the next full moon. I'm tired of marrow and tubers only!"

That immediately set off a wave of whispering through the band. More than a few nodded in agreement with Lu. So far, not good.

"Funny you should say that," Uru responded after taking a bite out of a tuber. "I was going to ask everyone if they would be alright with staying here for a bit longer."

The way everyone else in the band stared at her, one would have thought she had cursed all their ancestors loud enough for the whole world to hear.

"Have you lost all your senses, Uru?" Lu asked. "We can't stay here for even one more moon. We're running out of meat. If we haven't already."

"I understand. But hear me out, even if it sounds a little crazy. Ever since Oja left, I've been having . . . visions of her whenever I sleep. She's been calling out to me in every one of them, telling me I have forsaken her. I believe it's a sign she's out there, waiting to be found."

"And that is why we were hoping the band would stay here at least a few days longer," Namak added. "Uru and I want to venture south to look for her. If the band is to move anywhere while we are gone, we will find ourselves as lost as her."

Lu's eyes rolled. "So you want us to starve while you're tracking down someone who ran away by her own choice. Isn't that so wise and selfless? Let her waste away in the bush, for all I care."

"Lu!" his father barked. "You and Oja might not have gotten along, but she is still your sister. And, if she is calling out to her friends through their dreams, then she must need their help."

Lu shook his head, digging in to challenge his father. "That's the thing, we don't know if she's calling out to Uru. Sometimes dreams mean nothing, or are sent by malign spirits to trick us. You can't always take them so seriously."

"But you cannot simply ignore them, either," old Kulro said. "If young Uru is having these visions every night she sleeps, they must be telling her something."

"I agree, but I think my son still has a good case for moving on," Yuke said. "Even if Oja needs Uru and Namak to rescue her, we can only wait for them so long. Never mind the game—I've found that even the tubers have become harder to find. I miss my daughter as much as any other mother would, but we cannot starve ourselves while we wait for her friends to bring her back."

"There's something you're all forgetting," Uru said, her tone sharpening, her irritation at their lack of concern for Oja growing. "The rains may be late, but they should be coming any week now. And when they do, they will bring forth the berries and fruit, and make the grass green so that more animals will come to graze. So even if Namak and I are gone for a long time, the band will have plenty to eat if they wait long enough."

"But what if the rains don't come soon?" Lu retorted. "What if they never return? Have you ever thought about that, Uru?"

"Since when have the rains never come at all?" Kulro asked. "They always come in the end. You're simply impatient as always, little Lu."

"Don't you dare call me *little* anymore, you old sack of bones!"

Lu lunged himself at Kulro with balled fists, but Aukah yanked his son back before the boy could do the elder any harm.

"Let us all have a vote," Aukah announced. "Those in favor of us staying in wait while Uru and Namak go off to find my daughter, raise your hand."

A few hands went up, but not enough for Namak's liking. The majority of the band kept their hands down. Uru and Namak fought back tears.

Aukah shook his head gently, his eyes glistening with disappointment in his band, concerned about the feelings of Oja's two best friends. "I am sorry, but you can see most want to leave. But I have another suggestion. Any in favor of heading south from here, closer to where my daughter might be?"

"But we don't know if there is water or game in the south," Lu said.

"That doesn't mean it isn't there, my son. Anyway, all those who wish to venture south, raise your hand."

Many more hands raised until they formed a little forest of affirmative arms around the fire. Finally, realizing he was hopelessly outvoted, Lu lifted his hand up after a final hesitant shrug.

Aukah's frown reversed into a smile directed at Uru and Namak. "Looks like we have a compromise. We'll leave tomorrow, but we shall go south. Uru, you and Namak can go looking for Oja while we are on the move. How does that sound?"

Uru and Namak bowed their heads toward him. "Thank you so much," Uru said.

Across the campfire, Lu scowled at them, the firelight blazing in his eyes.

CHAPTER TWELVE
Oja's Vision

Shards of rock blacker than charcoal jolted up like giant ribs from both edges of the valley. Oja felt those jagged protrusions had to be rock even though no light reflected on them that would reveal the coarse texture of stone. They might as well have been made of pure shadow.

There was no sound within the valley, not even the quietest whisper of the wind. Nor did there appear to be any trees, bushes, grass, or any other evidence of life. Between the twin walls of hills punctured with black precipices, there lay only boulders of the yellow rock that Nyzai, the chieftain of the Monitor people, had called gold. Oja saw so many such boulders; even the sand glittered at her feet. All she had to do was plunge her fingers into it, and she would come back with more than enough of the strange stone to satisfy the chieftain. All without the need for Bukti to protect her.

Just as well. He was nowhere to be seen. Neither were any ape-people lurking. Oja was alone in the silent landscape. She clawed at the sand with confident abandon, her fingers sparkling yellow as she gathered a ball of it. Between her cupped hands, the grains of gold congealed into a larger nugget. She smiled and laughed at her own reflection on its surface.

Oja blinked—and beheld the faces of Uru and Namak. "Why have you forsaken us, Oja?" her friends said together with resonant voices.

Oja dropped the nugget, which shattered back into grains of sand. When she scooped up another handful from the valley floor, the sand did not merge into another nugget. Instead, it melted into a thick liquid like yellow blood. And this time, her mother's and father's faces appeared within it.

"Why have you forsaken us?" they asked, the same tone to their plaintive echo as she'd just heard from Uru and Namak.

Oja recoiled back onto her feet, the fluid spilling from her hands. She shook her head in disbelief and astonishment. All the boulders in the valley turned into golden prisms, reflecting the faces of everyone from her bands: friends, family, neighbors, even Lu. All were calling out to her, their voices reverberant within the valley:

"Why have you forsaken us? Why have you forsaken us?"

Oja pressed her hands over her ears to shut out their cries, to no avail. "I have not forsaken you!" she yelled. "It's only that I cannot go back to you!"

The voices only multiplied in loudness as the valley trembled with every plaintive plea, every word. Outcroppings of gold rolled between the hills on both sides as the earth-shaking temblors intensified, until the boulders fed into the same valley and began tumbling after Oja like a stampede of buffalo.

As she ran for her life, the once flat valley floor tilted further downward until it grew a hard edge and became a cliff from which she fell. The gold boulders, bearing the likenesses of her former people, rained down after her, the faces reflected in their surfaces, reciting the same phrase with endless repetition:

"Why have you forsaken us? Why have you forsaken us? Why have you forsaken us, Oja?"

"I have not!" Oja screamed. "I will never forsake you! I will always remember—"

She opened her eyes and sprang up from her zebra-hide pallet, panting as beads of perspiration rose on her brow.

She cleared her senses, then her mind. Her eyes focused, the sight before her taking shape, clarity. She realized she was inside the hut Pok and his family had invited her into last night, as revealed by twilight's end casting its dim purple glow from outside. It was more spacious than Urjah's hut, with enough room to accommodate Pok and his two sons in addition to their guest. Oja was the only one awake, as her hosts were still snoring in deep sleep on pallets laid over the floor, their heads supported by curved wooden headrests.

Her mind began whirling. What did the dream mean? Was her band truly calling out to her, begging her to return? She'd assumed they considered her dead. Was this a trick by some malicious spirit to make her feel worse, as most nightmares were supposed to be? But if so, whose spirit would want her to think back to the people she had once called her own?

She might have made a mistake in joining these strangers who called themselves the Monitor people. Yet she didn't know of a way to return to her former band on the high plains, or even where they might be. By now, considering how much time had passed since she had left the camp, they undoubtedly would have packed up and headed somewhere else—but in which direction? And what was she to do if they were to continue haunting her dreams? Hopefully it would never happen again.

She did not dare go back to sleep.

Bukti's pallet ruffled under his weight as he rose to rub the back of his head and stretch his arms. "You look like you've been up for a while, Oja," he said, his voice low.

"Not that long before you," Oja replied. "I . . . had a bad dream, that's all."

"Oh, those are always nasty. At least you and I got up right on time. It's almost sunrise."

Bukti took down a basket hanging from the ceiling's thin log rafters and handed Oja a dried piece of doum palm fruit. She devoured it in a few chomps, her hunger taking charge, not even pausing to chew thoroughly.

"If that doesn't take your mind off your dream, nothing will," Bukti said. "How about we head out now? Best to get an early start before it gets too hot."

He picked up his spear from the pair of prongs on the wall on which it had been mounted. Oja gathered her bow, quiver, and knife from beside her. Bukti motioned with his head, and they snuck out of the hut into the cool, crisp air that awaited them outside. His eyes glimmered with concern as he looked back at Oja. "Is something troubling you? You don't seem that eager to go."

"It's not that," Oja said. "It's more like . . . do you have to go to the valley with me? After what you've seen me do?"

"Oja, you know my sister wanted me to come with you. If I were to stay here against her orders, she would crack my skull open. And, while you may have been able to kill that one crocodile in the river, that doesn't mean you could fend off a whole troop of ape-people by yourself."

"I could escape them. Or hide from them."

"And what will you do when you can't? That's where two are better than one. And, again, I'm only doing what my sister told me to do. You have a problem with what she said, you should have taken it up with her."

"So you have to do whatever one person tells you? You can't try to change her mind or have the people vote on it?"

Bukti gave her a blank stare. "What's a vote?"

Oja slapped her brow. "You don't know what voting is? Ugh, never mind. We'll wake everyone else up if we keep talking here."

They hurried down the avenue that ran through the village, from the northern slope of the mound which supported the Chieftain's hut until they passed through a tusked archway at the road's end, identical to the entrance that they had used to get into the village from the south the previous day. They vanished into the woods beyond, headed for the valley of gold.

CHAPTER THIRTEEN
Valley of the Ape-People

Shortly after daybreak, Oja and Bukti came upon another monolith impressed with the gold-striped lizard emblem of the Monitor people. This one did not stand straight up like the others, but instead leaned over a stream that gurgled southeastward through the woodland. Dangling on a rope from a post at its top was a skull bleached whiter than a cloud, its naked teeth clacking against one another in the breeze.

The skull was not that of a human being. The brows were too prominent, forming a double-arched bridge over the eyes, and the lower face protruded forward like a snout. It resembled the skull of a chimpanzee, Oja thought, but the hollow case of its absent brain was larger than a typical ape's, more on par with a human. There could be no confusing what creature the skull came from.

A chill raced down Oja's spine. Somehow, the brisk dawn air felt even colder.

"And so we enter the land of the ape-people," Bukti said. "Stay close behind, Oja. They could be anywhere."

Though she did not verbalize it, Oja bristled internally at the word "behind." As much as she needed Bukti to show her the way to the valley, she did not need him talking like he wanted to take charge of their journey. It was she who had to find the gold, after all, not him. It was her quest.

Still, it was better to be prepared for ape-people at all times, and to have someone familiar with them as her accomplice, so she took out her bow and restrung it.

After Oja and Bukti refreshed themselves with fresh flowing stream water, they trekked beside it against the flow of the current. As they advanced upcurrent, the land started to slope upward, albeit at a shallow angle, with the trees thinning along the way until they were confined to the very shores of the stream. Beyond that narrow area, the woods opened into scrubby grassland.

Despite the more exposed terrain and passage of the sun, the day had not grown as hot as Oja had expected. She could not see the sun or the sky at all. Instead, a thick gray layer of clouds hung over the earth, bathing everything below it in a shadow.

Wind moaned between the irregular fangs of granite that pierced up from both sides of the valley, with the branches of trees and shrubs scratching one another as they shook. Only the warmth Oja's body had generated within from all the trekking buffered her against the damp cold wind that buffeted her. And yet, uncomfortable as the biting wind was, she welcomed the change in weather. After so many moons of scorching-hot dryness, it was a sign that the rains were on their way.

If only her late grandmother could see this.

"We should find shelter," Bukti said. "It could pour any moment now."

Oja looked in all four directions. "Where would we find shelter? I don't see any caves around."

"There should be some further up the valley. The ape-people like to sleep in them."

"So, what if we find a cave? Will there be ape-people in it?"

Bukti shrugged his shoulders. "If so, we leave them alone, simple as that. We don't want to get into a fight unless we have to, like with any other animal."

Like with any other animal. So long as Oja remembered her encounter with the leopard on the high plains, the one event precipitating this wayward journey, she could not disagree with Bukti even if she wanted to.

She took another step—a cracking sound. Something dry and rough was beneath her foot.

Bone. Again. This time, a fractured skeleton, rather than one piece. She looked down to see ribs, limbs, vertebrae, and shards of another skull. Unlike the skull they had seen hanging from the monolith earlier, this looked fully human, without any ape-like facial features whatsoever.

Bukti laid his fingertips on the brow of the broken skull. "This could have been Joru, the young son of my father's sister. He went hunting with his friends out here many rains ago, but they came back without him. They said they lost sight of him somehow."

"Why were they hunting in the valley of ape-people?" Oja asked. "Wouldn't they have known of the danger that's supposed to be here?"

"Everywhere outside the village has danger, and I will guess that they wanted to look brave to everyone else."

After poring over the bones, Bukti squinted at a straight, shallow indentation that ran across the left femur. "See that cut mark? He must have been butchered like an impala for meat. Many beasts may eat the flesh of humans, but I know of only one that butchers them that way."

"Ape-people?"

Bukti nodded silently, tears forming in his eyes. He tried to shield them from Oja's sight.

Lying on the ground next to the skeleton was a flat, fist-sized rock with faded traces of dried blood on its sharpened edge. Oja's stomach twisted inside her as she imagined how a vicious ape-person would have used this crude handheld blade.

Bukti's knuckles jutted as he squeezed onto the shaft of his spear, a spark of anger in his tears. "May the ape-people be cursed forever."

The further up the valley they traveled, the steeper and less even the land became. The stream at the bottom shrank in width until it amounted to little more than a fissure with foamy water trickling over it. Large outcroppings of rock strewn over the valley floor became more numerous as well, some so large they rivaled sleeping elephants or rhinoceroses in size. Several times, Oja needed to check boulders twice to make sure she had not confused them with those mighty animals, well remembering her surprise encounter with a rhinoceros she had mistaken for a boulder and barely escaping with her life as a result.

The scene started to resemble the valley in her dream, except the giant hunks offered nothing but dull gray stone rather than shimmering gold. Not once during their hike had she spotted any other piece of yellow material coveted by the Monitor people, the substance Nyzai had tasked her to find, not even the smallest grain.

The cloud cover still blocked the sun from sight, so Oja could only guess whether it had risen to its midday zenith. Either way, the day had barely warmed up at all. If anything, it had grown cooler as the clouds gradually shifted to a darker, more ominous shade of gray.

Through the shrill wail of the wind, they heard the soft grumble of faraway thunder. Afterward, something yelped like a startled child.

Near the opposite bank of the stream from Oja and Bukti, an ape-woman hugged her infant tight, her arms covered in fluffy hair, tightly coiled like a human being's. As her youngster squealed, the mother hummed and murmured gentle endearments into its ears much as Oja's mother would have comforted her during every thunderstorm when she was little. Even the way the ape-woman stroked the baby's head with one hand was human-like to an eerie, strangely heart-gnawing degree.

All her life, Oja had heard the ape-people described and recognized by Aukah and the entire band as the eternal enemies of humankind, continuously battling her people over food and foraging grounds the way lions and hyenas fought tooth and claw over each other's kills. Never had she considered that the ape-people, too, would feel such love and express such for their children, even though that was the instinctive way of mothers among the vast majority of creatures, especially those with warm blood running through their bodies. She always envisioned them as hateful brutes, without any capacity to feel love or tenderness, with humans like her band and Bukti's people the only beings capable of expressing such feelings.

The ape-woman noticed her unwelcome intruders. She turned her head to Oja and Bukti, and the loving eyes with which she watched her baby flared. She curled her lips back, baring her teeth, and screeched in the tone of pure menace before she ran off with her ape-child against her breast.

"We should hurry on," Bukti said. "She'll warn the rest of the tribe that we're here. We don't want them to track us down."

"Where in this big valley do we find the gold, anyway?" Oja asked. "I've tired of all the walking."

Bukti smiled at her. "Don't worry, we're almost there."

He had spoken the truth. After they sped to a near-gallop, neither one daring to glance over their shoulders to where they had seen the ape-woman, it was not long before they found a cave yawning like a lion's maw in the hills east of the stream. An upturned rock before one corner of the cave's entrance bore a circle painted in gold. Resting upon it was a wooden shaft, with a semicircular blade of basalt hafted onto it.

"That symbol on the rock means there's gold in there," Bukti said. He picked up the strange tool and handed it to Oja. "And this would be a pickaxe, so we can dig it out. I'll make a fire inside so you can see."

A wet prickle landed on Oja's skin. All around, thin droplets of water dropped on the valley, staining the soil beneath their feet with dark dots.

"You don't have much time," Oja said. "Soon all the wood will be too damp to burn."

She rushed into the cave as the drizzle thickened, ducking her head beneath the blunt knobs of stone that projected downward from the ceiling. As her vision adjusted to the darkness, she found the floor covered with rock fragments, some big as fists, others reduced to grains. These must have been broken off the walls. But Oja could find no gold among them.

After a few hard clacks, a firelight blossomed from behind her to brighten the interior. The pile of grass and sticks that Bukti had gathered for the tinder was barely bigger than a pair of cupped hands, so she would have to dig out her gold in as little time as she could while the rain poured down outside.

Oja stabbed and scraped at the cave wall with the sharp tip of the pickaxe blade. She struck not the solid rock she had expected upon first sight, but rather softer, porous soil that crumbled to the tool's touch. Again she struck at the wall, tearing away more of the reddish-brown earth with each stroke until it accumulated into a pile next to her feet.

Bukti clapped. "You're doing well for your first time!"

After she struck more blows against the cave wall, a soft yellow gleam finally emerged from the sediment. Oja dropped her pickaxe and clawed out the nugget with her fingers, laughing with glee as she held it in her palm.

Bukti peered over her shoulder, flashing a less-than-enthusiastic expression between a thin grin and a frown. "That's a small one."

"What?" Oja snapped. "Your sister never said it had to be a big nugget. This should be enough for her. Gold is gold, isn't it?"

"I would dig some more just in case. You could come home with two nuggets, or more."

Frustrated by him, Oja groaned and then went back to her work. She attacked with more fury than before, hacking out hunks of earth long after she had bored a deep gash into the cave wall. The noise of her intense excavation rivaled the amplified volume of the hiss and patter of the rain outside.

The pickaxe struck something hard, the sensation vibrating into her hands, wrists, and arms. She stopped and looked down. Another lump of gold, but this one was bigger than the first. She pried it out, her victorious laughter interwoven with exhausted panting. If this second nugget did not impress Bukti or Nyzai, nothing would.

"I've got one. We can leave," she exclaimed.

Oja turned to show him what she had found. He was not by the fire anymore. She scanned the cave, alarmed, finding him in a hunched posture back at the mouth of the cave, his spear pointed outward as he gripped it with both hands.

"What's the matter?" Oja asked.

He thrust his finger outward. "Ape-men."

She squinted through the sheets of rain outside and spotted them. The hirsute creatures squatted beneath a stunted tree on the other side of the stream, watching the cave as they clutched clubs of wood and bone.

"We must leave," Oja said. "Escape before they can chase us."

Bukti shook his head. "Not in this rain. We'll slip on the mud."

Oja looked behind her and checked the fire. It had already died down, with only a sprinkle of dim embers. Likewise, all warmth and light fled from the cavern interior, a frigid blackness quickly filling in the empty space.

"If we don't go now, they'll corner us here," Oja said. "We can move carefully so that we don't slip."

Bukti shrugged. "It's worth a try."

They snuck out of the cave and into the rain, breaking into a jog and holding the steady, rhythmic pace as they moved down the valley. Their feet squished over slick mud and wet grass, but the precipitation had thinned just enough to see into the distance. They found the quicker pace less exhausting heading down the grade than it had been hiking uphill all morning.

A simian screech chopped through the wind, chilling Oja to her marrow. Behind her and Bukti, the troop of ape-men poured forward, brandishing their wood and bone clubs while shrieking at their quarry with a blood hatred cultivated by generations of rivalry between their kind and humanity. The shaggy brutes were gaining ground with alarming rapidity over the soggy terrain.

Something whizzed through the rain and smacked the back of Bukti's head, knocking him off his feet. He tumbled down the slope until he collided into a boulder, the ape-men quickly catching up and assembling into a ring that enclosed their victim. Bestial hunger as well as rage flamed in the monsters' red eyes as they started pounding his body with their crude weapons, drenching their edges with his blood.

Screaming out Bukti's name, Oja ripped out her bow and shot an arrow into one of the ape-men, taking him out. Once the rest of the troop noticed their comrade's sudden death, they charged her, leaving the fallen Bukti behind. As Oja sprinted down the valley, she stopped for brief moments once, twice, three times to fire arrows at her pursuers, felling them one by one. She slayed half the troop by the time the leader of the ape-men tossed its weapon aside and reversed course with panicked screaming, its companions following suit.

After the last creature disappeared from sight, she crouched behind a shrub, waiting for Bukti to recover and reemerge. The rain passed, sunlight arrowing through the clouds at last, but he had yet to return to her. Her worries grew increasingly heavy with every passing moment. Finally, Oja ran back up the valley to where he had fallen. Once she arrived, she found only bloodstains on the grass.

Bukti was gone. The ape-men must have carried him off while retreating. They had no use for human prisoners, so no doubt the brutes would celebrate with a feast, the main course being poor Bukti. He seemed fated to meet the same end as his cousin Joru, butchered and devoured.

She may have obtained the gold she needed, but this was no time to celebrate. Dropping onto her knees, Oja cried out to the ancestors, praying that they would accept Bukti's spirit among them. She had known him only a few days, but his passing felt as if a part of her world was being torn out, emptying it even further. Like how she had felt upon Urjah's passing.

Even after the sun returned to bestow its heat upon the land, Oja shivered while she made her way back down the valley.

CHAPTER FOURTEEN
Return to the Village

The sun did not stay up for long. It had already dipped itself behind the treetops to Oja's left by the time she reentered the riverside woodland from the valley. As shadows covered the undergrowth, growing blacker with each passing breath, she would have to tread with caution, even with the ape-people far behind.

The hairy monsters must have finished gorging on Bukti's corpse by now. She tried to shake such a gruesome vision from her mind, but could not. The feeling of the vision polluted Oja's insides with bile that weakened her at the core.

The dampness in the air from the earlier rainfall aggravated the chill of dusk even more than usual. Or maybe it was her anticipation over what she would have to tell the chieftain Nyzai, and their father, Pok, about Bukti's fate. Would the chieftain even let Oja become one of the Monitor people if she came back without Bukti? Gold or no gold? Nyzai did not seem like the understanding type, especially when outsiders were concerned. And especially when she was about to learn she'd lost her brother.

Nonetheless, Oja could not hide what happened to her companion. Lying to the chieftain about it would only dig a deeper pit for herself. Sooner or later, every untruth a person could tell would be uncovered and make things worse for them. Oja's mother, to whom she had falsely promised never to leave their camp alone, knew that already. Oja's deception hung over her like a heavy cloud.

Oja spotted the village's northern entrance right in the middle of sunset, the luster of sunlight dimming on its great ivory tusks. She stood in hesitation one pace in front of it, marveling at how the construction seemed to tower higher than before. The fear that the entrance, through some spontaneous accident, would crash down on her head at the exact moment she walked underneath it flickered in her mind.

Once she mustered enough courage to pass through it, it stayed still. Oja's heartbeat calmed after that quick spike.

At least the village smelled better than it had the day she first entered. The smoky odor hovered in the air as before, but this time it mixed with the more appetizing scents of meat, fish, and vegetables cooking as the people prepared their evening meals. Oja's mouth turned moist inside, reminding her that she and Bukti had not stopped to eat once during the day's hike. How she could go for a whole, juicy haunch of gazelle at that moment!

But first, she had to meet with the chieftain.

As with the entrance, the mound supporting Nyzai's hut loomed higher than before, almost like a mountain of earth. With a sigh, Oja squeezed her hands together behind her back as she walked up its ramp, whispering desperate prayers that the chieftain would not be waiting. Nyzai could have been spending time with the rest of her family, or dealing with business elsewhere in the village, or whatever else occupied a chieftain's day when not sitting in front of their hut atop the mound.

When Oja set foot on the mound's summit after a climb that seemed longer than it was, she spotted the cat Yowh first. He was gnawing on the bones of a pouched rat when she knelt down to give his furry little head a rub. Yowh's purr sounded satisfied and grateful . . . so she hoped.

"For someone who's never had a cat before, you sure know how to treat them well," she heard Nyzai say.

The chieftain sat on a stool of baobab wood outside her elephant-bone hut, her headdress removed. She bit into a date from a basket beside her as Oja approached.

"Were you waiting for me and Bukti all day up here?" Oja asked. "Your backside must be sore from all that sitting."

Nyzai chuckled. "More like I have a gift for knowing when you would be back. Though, I must admit, I had not counted on Bukti not showing up with you tonight." The smile on the chieftain's face, already vague, disappeared.

"That is . . . what I was going to tell you about. He fell to the ape-people in that valley."

Nyzai averted her eyes from Oja, her body shaking with a buildup of emotion. "I thought that would happen. You outsiders always bring bad luck, even more so those like you who wander the high plains. Tell me, did you make them attack you?"

"No! They found us and chased us down. I was able to fend them off, and kill many of them, but only after they attacked Bukti. After the rest of them fled, I raced back to Bukti to help him escape, but they must have taken him away while fleeing from me. You must understand, I did nothing to anger them. Please, Chieftain, you cannot blame me for his loss. Remember, it was you who had him go with me!"

Nyzai snarled. "Oh, so you would rather blame me? I wanted him to protect you. And you, you had to . . ."

The chieftain slammed her fist onto her thigh with a growl. Afterward, she inhaled deeply through her nose, calming herself, murmuring something, slowly easing her temper.

"So am I not wanted in your village?" Oja asked, holding up the nugget she had excavated from the cave between her fingers. "Even though I did find your gold? What do these strange yellow rocks mean to your people, anyway?"

"They are the blood of the sun, our mother," Nyzai said. "Those who find a drop of the sun's blood are her chosen. I suppose that, since you have found your gold, you can call yourself one of us now."

Oja's people had always seen the sun as their mother too, as well as the one in whom their ancestors would dwell after leaving the world of the living. She should have expected that these people of the river villages, different as their way of life was from her own, would regard the sun with the same filial reverence.

"Yet I will keep my eye on you, Oja," Nyzai went on. "If you so much as offend our ways, I will have you thrown out with no regrets."

Oja prostrated herself before the chieftain as she remembered Pok doing the day before. As she did so, she looked up to Nyzai with a wet shimmer pouring out of her eyes. "Thank you, O Chieftain. I owe you my thanks, and I am so sorry I could not save your brother."

Nyzai sighed. "You are forgiven . . . for now."

"Alright . . . so, now that I am of the Monitor people, should I move into the hut of your family down below? Or would it be better if I built a hut of my own somewhere else in your village?"

"Neither of those will be necessary. I have a place for you already."

"What place?"

"It's a special place, for a special type of person. A person I can keep my eye on at all times."

Oja cocked her eyebrow with arms crossed.

"Oh, don't worry, it's a place you will enjoy, and one you'll do well in," Nyzai continued. "How, Oja, would you like to be . . . our new hunt-leader?"

"Hunt-leader? What does that mean?"

"He—I should say, *they*—are the one who leads our hunters, as you should be able to tell from the name. Of course, it is normally a man who becomes our hunt-leader. But, since you were able to slay a crocodile as well as fend off those ape-people in the valley, saving one of my brothers and *almost* saving the other, it seems to me that you'll be as good for the role as any man."

"Wait, if you need a new hunt-leader, what happened to the old one?"

"A hippopotamus killed him not long before you came to our village. He was my husband, Erku. We even had a daughter together, but she died in my womb. I still think about them every day, as I will my brother Bukti."

Nyzai turned her head to face the last remaining sunlight in the sky. Watching her brought an ache to Oja's chest, a deep sadness and compassion, the first she felt for the chieftain. The poor woman had suffered enough loss in her life, with her husband, daughter, and brother now having ventured to the realm of the ancestors within the sun's radiant embrace.

"I am sorry for all the loved ones you have lost," Oja said. "At least I can always find another husband," Nyzai replied. "Now, let me show you to your new home, hunt-leader Oja."

She stood up from her stool and led Oja down the ramp behind her hut. After rounding the base of chieftain's mound toward the northwest, they approached another hut that, though not as massive as the chieftain's, still dwarfed its neighbors by at least a third. In front of it lay a broad yard of earth with corners marked by posts, leopards' skulls on top. The skull and mane of a lion was mounted over the hut's entryway.

"This yard is where you will train the younger hunters and hold meetings," Nyzai said. "Tomorrow, when I announce your appointment, you can expect all the hunters in the village to be gathered here to meet you. I would get some rest as soon as you can tonight. You've had a big day, and another one awaits you once the sun returns. In the meantime, hand me your gold and your necklace."

Oja caressed the turquoise amulet hanging from her necklace of teeth and ostrich-eggshell beads, which she had worn ever since her mother had given it to her as a child. It would be the last visible link Oja had to her former way of life. She dropped that along with the gold nugget into Nyzai's hand in an instant. She would give it up to become one of the Monitor people.

After Nyzai bade her good night, Oja staggered into the sprawling hut, her new home. Against its far wall inside rested a variety of spears, blades and clubs of stone, bone, and ivory, and arrows in quivers, but she was too tired to do more than glance at them. She dropped onto a soft pallet of lion manes in the center of the hut's interior and drifted off to sleep in little time.

CHAPTER FIFTEEN
The Search Begins

When daylight returned once again, it was not with the fiery brilliance of sunrise as before. It arrived dim and gray through a thick mist that cloaked the high plains. The earth, still damp and mucky from a day of rain, stuck itself onto the soles of Uru's feet while dewy grass licked her calves as she waded through it.

After enduring a dry season that lasted more moons than usual, she welcomed the sensation of moisture. If more rains followed, the trees would sprout fruit again and the grass would turn green and supple, inviting more herds to graze. No longer would Uru, Namak, and the other hunters have to venture far and wide for game while the rest of the band dug for tubers. As long as this new season lasted, they would find plenty of meat and sweet fruit to gorge upon.

Now they prayed that the rains would fall on the land for as long as they had been delayed.

Uru and Namak left camp the moment the last of the stars started fading back into the sky, while everyone else slept in their shelters. They needed as much time to search as they could muster, so it was better to get up and leave early. This time, they were not hunting for game—but for Oja. They glided southward across the high savanna in hopes of finding where it gave way to the lowlands, where she would await them.

So far, they had not found that point, either as a gentle downward slope or a steep drop like the ravine into which Oja had apparently fallen. Uru peered as far as she could through the mist. The plain rolled and rolled on, every bit as flat as it had been before. It did not make sense. How could the edge of the world be so close the other day but so far away now?

She heard a rapid succession of soft squelches on the ground. Uru and Namak halted to survey the fog surrounding them, fingers clasping tight on their spears. It could have been an animal moving about, such as a galloping antelope. Or a predator on the hunt, one that would require more stealth from them. Perhaps it was even a human being. But who? What would they be doing away from camp? Was it perhaps Oja? If so, how did she scale the distance in elevation between the high plains and the lowlands?

"Who's out there?" Namak called out.

She heard nothing but her echo. Not even more strange footsteps. Only the croaking of frogs and chirping insects. Uru squinted at the nearest patch of bushes, studying every leaf to make sure someone—or something—was not watching back. She saw nothing.

They resumed their trek, pulling closer together than before. If there really was something stalking them, they had to be prepared, which meant depending on each other for protection. Uru wondered if they should have brought someone else with them. Maybe Lu or his friend Tukar, although neither seemed particularly excited by the suggestion that Oja was still out there.

With the progression of day, the mist thinned until it no longer blocked out the sun and sky. The heat rose as well, but instead of the dry and dusty heat that had baked the savanna before yesterday's rain, a sweltering mugginess took an even more oppressive hold. Droplets of moisture hung in the air, intermingled with the perspiration that flowed down Uru's brow, stinging her eyes.

By the mercy of fate, she and Namak chanced upon a thin brook that wound like a serpent of water through the grass. Upon hearing its trickle, both women rushed to its shore and splashed it onto their faces, finally drinking in great gulps. Borne from the recent rainfall, the water from the brook was cooler and sweeter than any they had drunk recently. Such a welcome relief.

Wait, Uru thought. Rivers this fresh always flowed downhill. If she and Namak were to follow it, they might find their way to the lowlands and Oja after all.

They raced alongside the brook in the direction of its flow, their stamina rejuvenated by the relief it gave them. Ever so slightly, the land started to slope downward, even if it was at an angle too subtle to notice without observing the stream and its many little cataracts. Uru wanted it to remain that way the whole journey, without her and Namak needing to go down any cliffs or ravines.

After following for a while, she pulled up disappointed: the brook ended at the edge of a big hole in the ground. It was so big that a herd of elephants would not be enough to cover its opening.

Nor was it shallow. It bored into the earth blacker than midnight, not even the dimmest spark of light visible from the bottom—if it had any bottom at all. Uru always imagined the deep interior of the world glowed red with molten rock, like mountains to the far west sometimes spewed from their summits, yet she could not see anything like that down there.

"You want to dive in?" Namak asked, the corner of her mouth pulled up in a half-smirk.

Uru gulped. "We could light a torch and throw it down there to see how deep it is."

Behind them, the grass rustled. Before Uru could turn to look behind her, a hard wooden stick smacked the small of her neck, batting her into the blackness below. And Namak was falling and screaming alongside her.

As he watched the darkness of the pit swallow up the two women, Tukar's heart sank beneath the weight of his conscience while the stick slipped out of his grasp.

He had always liked Uru and Namak, and not only because they were reliable hunters for their band. Both were attractive young maidens like their friend Oja, although neither had shown any more interest in him than she had. Never had he wanted to inflict any harm upon them, or Oja, for that matter. This was Lu's idea. He was the one who wanted them gone.

Nearby, Lu sneered with triumph as he tapped the palm of his hand with his stick. Not even the slightest glimmer of regret flashed from the little jackal's eyes.

"What are we going to tell the band?" Tukar asked.

"It won't be hard at all," Lu said. "They fell into that sinkhole by accident. Maybe lions or hyenas chased them into it. No one's going to bother following the tracks to find out what really happened, will they?"

"But what if they do? What would your mother and father think?"

"They'll come around to see the wisdom of my decision. Don't you see that Oja was a threat to our people? If her foolishness hadn't gotten her stranded, and now searching for her instead of what we really need—fresh meat—she would have gotten one of us killed sooner or later. She has no place among us."

"And what of Uru's and Namak's families? If they find out the truth, they'll never forgive you—or me."

Lu shook his stick at Tukar, growling through bared teeth. "Shut up, or you'll join those two down there! You will not speak of it. Nor will I. Not another word. Nobody will find out. You hear? Trust me on that!"

Tukar had no desire to argue with his longtime friend, and even less to challenge that ruthless side of him. *His own sister? Her best friends? While they searched for their missing friend?* He could only shrug and grunt. He peered one last time into the gaping, almost bottomless black hole before he and Lu headed back to camp, with a sound he had heard earlier echoing through his brain like in a frightful dream.

It had been a couple of faint, yet reverberant splashes coming from deep in that hole.

Namak should have expected water at the bottom of the hole—once they finally landed with firm plops. *If only whoever hit us could hear us land, maybe they'd realize the hole wasn't really bottomless, think twice about what they did, and try to pull us out.* If there was a stream of water feeding the bottom of the hole, then over time it would collect into a pool, possibly swelling toward the top after repeated rains.

What she had not counted on was the current that carried her deeper into the darkness. When she floated back up to the water's surface, she could not even see the opening of the hole into which she and her friend had fallen. Blackness surrounded and engulfed her in all directions, blacker than the darkest night. The cold water grasped and chilled her body, the cool brush of drafty air further cooling her wet face, but she could see nothing.

Behind her, or possibly before or beside her, she heard Uru surface and gasp for air.

"We must be in the underworld," Namak said.

After a few moments, Uru caught her breath. "You think we'll meet any wicked souls? I sure can't hear anyone but us."

"Maybe they don't make any noise."

It was a guess as reasonable as any other. The souls of the wicked, those who did not deserve to return to the sun's embrace after their passing, were known to strike disease into anyone without warning. If they never made sounds when they visited the realm of the living, they could be every bit as silent in their native abode below the earth.

"Well, I don't feel sick, either," Uru said.

"Then we should stay quiet, lest they hear us," Namak said.

After her eyes adjusted to the otherwise sheer blackness, she noticed the braids of Uru's hair sparkle against a pale green light.

Above their heads, mushrooms glowed like luminescent gemstones from a coarse ceiling of limestone, opening to the contours of a vast subterranean tunnel half-filled by the river which had carried them there. Long, conical daggers of rock stabbed down from the ceiling and also up from the water's surface, some merging into one another at the tips to form natural columns. Only the dripping of water from the upper stalactites punctuated the silence within this enormous vault.

Something tickled Namak's calves. She looked down in the clear water to see a school of tiny fish, all of which gave off pale blue light as brilliant as that of the mushrooms. The creatures darted away from a larger fish that pursued them in hungry thrusts, rows of luminous dots running down its flank. Namak sighed: so there was a whole world of light in this darkest of darkness after all!

"This part of the underworld is prettier than I would have thought," Uru said.

"So what do you think knocked us down that pit?" Namak asked. "I'm thinking it was that little creeper, Lu. I could tell he never liked his sister."

"But enough to keep us from bringing her back? And to kill us? Why?"

The current gained force and speed again, pushing them down the river and through the massive cavern faster. The further they floated downstream, the louder the hissing roar of water pouring down from another height . . . perilously close to them . . .

There was no more light to show the way when Namak felt herself falling through the air again.

CHAPTER SIXTEEN
The New Hunt-Leader

It took a whiff of roasted fish to drag Oja out of the realm of dreams.

The fish, together with some dried dates and a clay cup of milky-white liquid, lay on the semicircular frond of a palmyra palm on the floor right beside her headrest, revealed by the sunlight that blasted through her new hut's entryway. The sunlight was much too bright for it to be the earliest hours after darkness. Her exhaustion from the day before must have sunk her into her deepest sleep despite the groaning of her hunger pangs.

After murmuring thanks to whomever had laid the meal before her, she did not hesitate to gobble it up, nor did she even pause to savor any of its flavors. She quickly finished and then downed the drink in a single swig. It was sweet and tangy to her tongue, yet left a burning sensation within her like nothing she had ever drunk before. Still, it was enough to moisten her gullet.

She looked down and noticed her necklace resting next to where the consumed food and drink once laid. Only, instead of her old turquoise amulet serving as the center stone, there twinkled the gold nugget she had dug up in the valley. She placed it around her neck, a tear forming in her eye, saddened by the life it cost for her to return with it.

Outside, she saw the shadows of human figures, murmuring and whispering to one another. Those must have been the hunters Nyzai had arranged to meet their new leader. *If so*, Oja thought, *I've kept them waiting long enough.* Men, if they were all men, were never known for their patience.

She sprang up and burst out to a thick wall of bodies in the court before her hut, glistening with sweat from the muggy heat of an encroaching midday. All appeared to be men, their arms crossed and mouths curved down into unwelcoming frowns. A young and short man at the front scowled even more fiercely than the rest, brandishing a pair of stitched scars where his nipples should have been and hips wider than normal for a male human. Was he one of those men who had been born into the bodies of women? Oja had heard of people being born into the body of the wrong sex, but never had she encountered one before.

The man was first to address her. "What took you so long, woman?" he demanded, speaking with a throaty deepness that contrasted with the feminine edge to his voice.

"'Woman? Is that how you address me?" Oja asked. "Your chieftain chose me to lead the hunters. I ask that you treat me with the same respect you treat her."

"Why so? A woman can lead a village from the safety of her hut, but can she hunt with a man's strength and courage?"

Oja snarled and gritted her teeth. "Listen, young boy, I can tell you were born into a woman's body. You're not one to tell me I have no strength!"

All the men in the assembly gasped. The one who had spoken clenched his fists nearly tight enough for his knuckles to pop through his skin. "How dare you!"

Oja pointed down to his skirt with a mischievous smirk. "I bet you still have a womb instead of a manly shaft down there, don't you?"

"Stop it, you two!" an older man in the audience said. "Hunt-leader, our brother Kore was wrong to attack your womanhood, but neither should you mock his manhood."

Oja and the man called Kore said nothing more, instead exchanging glinting glares at one another while inhaling through their nostrils. Kore stepped back into the crowd, an inaudible grumble behind his closed lips.

"Don't mind Kore," the man next to him said while patting his shoulder. "When you are born with the body of a woman like him, you try to make up for it as much as you can."

Kore pulled himself sideways from the other man with a disapproving squint but no further comment.

Oja was done entertaining that line of conversation. "We leave this talk behind us. As your chieftain has told you, I will be your new hunt-leader. I may be a woman, but I was born on the high plains, where women and men both hunt. I can hunt as well as any of you."

"Is that so?" a stout and stocky man in the crowd asked. "How did you come here from the high plains anyway?"

Oja wished she had foreseen that awkward question coming. If she were to tell the story of her and the rhino, or the leopard and the gazelle before that, these men would never follow her on a hunt. They might even protest to their chieftain, who would then swipe away the very responsibility she had bestowed upon Oja. What would happen to her then?

She forced herself to reply, "It is a long story. I will not bore you by telling it all."

"Bore us?" Kore said. "You need not worry about boring us, woman. You're hiding something, aren't you?"

There was no use for Oja to withhold the truth any longer. Or at least not one scrap of it. "It . . . was an accident. We—no, I—was hunting a rhinoceros, and it drove me off a cliff into the river that flows all the way to here."

"You were hunting that rhino by yourself?" Kore nodded, the edge lifting from his voice, the snarl leaving his face. Along with some doubt. "I see you have a man's courage after all, woman—if not truly a man's sense."

Oja had already grown tired of Kore's barbs against her gender. "It's not only men who can have courage, whether or not they also have sense. As long as I am your hunt-leader, you will not insult my womanhood anymore. Or any women. Understood?"

A fierceness blazed in Kore's eyes. The fierceness of a challenge laid down. "How will you keep me from doing so, woman?"

As much as she sizzled with the desire to pounce on Kore and slash him apart with her fingernails like a leopard, Oja knew she could not lash out at any villagers on impulse, or Nyzai would have her cast out forever. Still, she had to teach the little gnat to show some respect.

She reflected back to the boy the same wicked expression he'd given her. "We'll use you as bait next time we go after a lion, leopard, or crocodile. How does that sound?"

The rest of the men snickered like giddy hyenas, the one next to Kore slapping him on the back. Kore recoiled with a somewhat embarrassed cringe as he turned his gaze away from Oja.

Another man, this one tall and wiry, raised his hand. "Kore does ask one good question, though: How do we know you can hunt? None of us have seen a woman hunt before."

"I will show you," Oja said. "The rains started to fall yesterday, did they not? We could welcome them with a feast, as my people do on the high plains. Why not hunt for meat?"

"But if you want to feed the whole village, you will need something with a lot of meat on it," the stout man said. "Like an elephant or rhinoceros."

Oja nodded, considering the man's reasonable comment. "How about a hippopotamus? You people live by the river. There should be plenty of them close by."

The men looked at one another, blinking as they whispered bits of disbelief among themselves. Kore shook his head with crossed arms while rolling his eyes. "Have you ever hunted a hippo before, woman?" he asked. "Or anything bigger than a rat?"

"I've taken down many antelope and zebras, not to mention a crocodile," Oja said. "While rescuing one of your own from its jaws."

"The zebra?" Kore asked. That got a burst of laughter from the men.

"No, the crocodile. I rescued the chieftain's brother when he brought me here."

Silence from the crowd. Kore shook his head, uncertain whether to believe her, but unwilling to make a further fool of himself.

"Of course," Oja continued, "a hippo would require more hunters, but that's where you all come in. If we work together, we can bring anything down. It shouldn't matter whether I am a man or a woman."

The stout man in the audience nodded. "What you say makes sense. But you should know you cannot simply leap out of the tall grass and charge at a hippo with your spear and come out alive. You'll need a plan of some kind."

Oja nodded. "That won't be hard. Once we scout for the nearest hippo herd, we'll think of a way to draw one out and attack it. How does that sound?"

The tall and wiry man scratched the scruffy hair on his chin. "Well, it's not much of a plan yet, but sometimes you need to be there to know what to do." He turned to the full group of hunters. "I say we follow her anyway. What do you say, men?"

Slowly and gradually, little by little, nearly all of the men raised their hands, nodding in agreement, ready to follow her on this hunt to see if she spoke the truth. The one exception was Kore, but within a minute, he succumbed to the consensus with a groan and raised his hand too.

Oja smiled. "Good. Thank you. Then hippo it shall be. We must get ready as soon as we can."

CHAPTER SEVENTEEN
Escape from the Underworld

Another hard smack, another hard splash into darkness. This one hurt Uru less than before, the drop shorter and less severe, but still, it was not something she cared to experience a second time. How deep into the underworld did this river flow? Would it ever take her and Namak to the lowlands, or would it bring them even deeper into the bowels of the earth? Did this river have an end at all? Where did rivers end, anyway?

Uru heard a resurfaced Namak spew out a mouthful of water, some of which fell onto her shoulder.

"If there really are any souls down here, we should ask them about the way out," Namak said. "If there is a way out at all."

A little further down the river, total blackness gave way to another spattering of the luminous fungi on the cavern ceiling. The light they cast revealed a low, stony bank that slanted up from the water's edge to Uru's left. She and Namak swam toward the bank until they could wade out. Cold and dripping wet, it brought a small relief to stand on dry land once more.

What was less pleasant was the permeating odor of ordure. Tiny pellets of it were littered all over the cave floor, and Uru could not stand anywhere without squishing her feet over them.

"Ugh, whose shit would this be?" she asked.

Namak placed her finger on her lips with a "Shh . . ." while pointing to the ceiling. Overhead, a crowd of bats slept upside down, wings wrapped around their bodies, hanging from the ceiling, giving them the appearance of cocoons growing downward. One squeaked as if the women's voices had awakened it for a quick moment . . . or perhaps it was only yawning.

"If there are bats, there must be a way out after all," Uru whispered. "Bats need to fly out every night."

A tunnel bored through the limestone away from the bank, lit by the mushrooms that sprouted between the roosting bats. Uru and Namak tiptoed down the passageway, careful to plant their feet as far away from pellets of guano as possible. The less they squished into the dung, the less likely they would disturb the creatures' slumber.

Something clattered over the floor. Uru halted and unslung her spear, her pulse accelerating.

"It was me," Namak said. "My foot kicked a bone."

They looked down, and found not one bone, but a pile lying against the tunnel wall. They studied the remains. Gazelle, by the look of the horned skull that lay among them. Shreds of decayed meat clung to the bones, emanating a stink even more intense than that of the guano.

"It couldn't have just died here," Namak said. "Something must have brought it in."

"Bats don't bring gazelle carcasses into their caves," Uru replied. "What could it have been?"

"Whatever made those."

Namak pointed to the cave floor, where footprints indented squashed guano, footprints unlike what she and Uru had left behind, not shaped like human feet at all. They looked more like feline paw prints a leopard or lion would leave behind. Some ran toward and away from the gazelle bones.

The insides of the earth felt even colder to Uru than before, especially on her back, to the point where her spine chilled.

Both women continued down the tunnel, their spears now out, sticking close together while maintaining the quietness of their approach, as not to awaken the bats above. They came to a spot where the underground corridor forked into two, neither of which terminated with any light other than that of the mushrooms. The paw prints continued down the path to the left.

"Should we go down the same way as the cat did?" Uru asked. "They might lead us to the way out."

"Or they might lead to wherever the cat still lurks," Namak said. "The other way would be safer."

"Fair enough."

They advanced down the path to the right, maintaining the same level of caution and silence as before. If there were fish, bats, and some sort of big cat living below the surface of the earth, Uru wondered, what else would she and Namak encounter on their way out? Was there a whole world of life here, one with people as well as animals managing to eke out an existence? If so, what kind of people? Hopefully they were human beings, or a people who could talk and reason like human beings, instead of grunting wild folk like the ape-people. If there were any of those horrible ape-people down there, they would be even less welcome company than whatever beast had left those tracks in the guano earlier. Especially since a troop of the brutes had killed Namak's father when she and Uru were little girls.

At last, a tiny pinpoint of white light pierced the darkness ahead like a solitary star. The closer they came, the more it expanded in brilliance, light finding its way into the darkness. They looked at each other, holding their breath, a hopeful leap in their hearts. It had to be an exit to this great cavern, where they could return to the sunlit world. And hopefully enter the lowlands where Oja would await their reunion.

They accelerated their pace to a jog, avoiding the piles of guano as much as they could. The light of the cave exit kept swelling in intensity until it almost blinded them. They hurried forward. It was only a matter of time before they would liberate themselves of the malodorous black hollows within the earth.

Just before the exit, Uru and Namak stopped in their tracks, paralyzed. Aghast. A black shadow stood in their way, a black shadow with twin yellow-green embers glaring back at them. The eyes of a beast.

Halfway between a lion and leopard in size, the cat in front of them had a stockier and brawnier build than either, with faint brown stripes and spots on its tawny hide. As it curled its lips back, it exposed drool-glossed upper fangs at least twice as long as the lower ones. This had to be one of the cats known as blade-fangs, Uru thought, the same blade-fangs that haunted the people and animals in mountains to the west. Never before had Uru or Namak seen one in the flesh. But to find one while leaving a deep cavern from the underworld?

The cat growled harshly at them. The two women stood still, withstanding its breath. It reeked of decayed flesh. More than sheer terror froze the huntresses in place. Uru's father had once told her that if you stood your ground in front of a predator rather than fleeing like prey, the predator would read it as a show of strength and back off without further threat or attack. The cat might not even be hungry, Uru remembered her father saying, but instead protecting its territory from rival hunters.

The blade-fang sank into a crouch, its muscles tensing under its fur, its ears pointed forward. Its eyes burned with carnivorous intent.

Uru and Namak stepped backward while jabbing their spears at the cat. It did not retreat. Instead, it hurled itself at Uru and slashed at her face. She dodged its claws with a backward tilt of her head, but the cat's paw nonetheless broke the shaft of her spear in half.

Their sleep shattered by the noise of the attack, the bats flew off their perches and fluttered in a raging swarm over the scene, harrying both the women and the blade-fang with their own small but sharp fangs and shrieking cries. While the cat was brushing bats away from itself with its forelegs, Uru and Namak raced past the bats and blade-fang both to escape into the sunlight and fresh air.

They looked quickly to the south. The savanna sprawled before them, trees and bushes growing in clusters that grew denser as they spread toward the horizon. There must have been a river or lake in the distance, Namak thought, possibly the very one Oja had fallen into. Behind them to the north rose rugged terraces of rock pitted with caves like the one they had left. There was no sign of a gentler slope or path leading from this new country back to the top.

For all that they knew, Uru and Namak had gotten themselves stranded the way Oja had. They could see no way of returning to their band from whatever land they were in now.

"There has to be someone down here who knows how to get back up those cliffs," Namak said.

Uru shook her head. "We'll look around, but I wouldn't bet any meat on it."

A feline roar rang from the north. Uru turned to find the blade-fanged cat hurtling at her again, its hide pocked with bleeding bite marks from the bats in the cave. It landed on her, pinning her down with its weight, its claws ravaging her skin while its hot saliva dripped onto her neck.

Wrestling her right arm free of the pressure from the blade-fang's paw, Uru punched it in the nose. This act of desperation yielded nothing but a retaliatory slap from the beast that scarred her cheek. Nor did kicking its underside with her knees get it off. The blade-fang's jaws gaped wide, unsheathing more of its namesake canines, as it readied to pierce her gullet.

With a shrill yowl, the cat tumbled off Uru at last, liberating her from its crushing weight. Namak stabbed it again in the flank, driving her spear deeply into the creature's body. The blade-fang let out one more croaking roar before it fell limp to the earth, its life departed to the realm of the dead.

Namak wiped perspiration off her brow. "At least we'll have some meat tonight. You will need a new spear, though, Uru."

CHAPTER EIGHTEEN
Roggan

Even after all the days since the crocodile pulled him from the canoe and bit him, Roggan's arm remained sore. As he lay on his pallet in his father's hut, he kept prodding it with his fingertips to make sure the beast's powerful jaws had not cracked the bone within it. So far, he felt nothing sharp underneath the skin and muscle, but he was no healer. Bukti knew the most about those things within the family, but from what Nyzai had told them the night before, Bukti was no more.

If only Roggan could join the other men in seeing the new hunt-leader. As it was, he only had Nyzai's word to go on.

Not that he minded that his sister had appointed Oja to lead the hunts from now on. He liked the newcomer, not merely because her physique was easy on the eyes, but also due to the courage and determination she had shown on the water. It was she who had slain the very crocodile that left his arm in ruin. If one must have a woman leading the hunts, best to be one like Oja.

It was a shame that, from what he remembered, she had shown more interest in Bukti when they met her further up the river. Though, as painful as Bukti's loss had been for the whole family, it did leave an opening that—

No, it was not right to think that way! His older brother's passing ripped a gaping hole from his life. There was nothing about it to celebrate, and doubtless Oja mourned Bukti's departure from the land of the living too. What she needed more than anything else was consolation. Maybe a gesture of compassion, to show her that he cared.

The pleasant smell of roasting tilapia streamed from outside the hut. Roggan rose up, his taste buds threatening to melt within his mouth, and walked to where his father cooked the fish on a spit of twigs. Nyzai was there too, without any of her chieftain's regalia. She sat cross-legged by the fire like another member of the family, supporting the cat Yowh on her legs while caressing the fur on his flank.

Roggan took his seat next to his big sister. "So how did the hunters receive Oja as their leader this morning?"

"Most of them, better than I expected," Nyzai said. "Though I know Kore is less happy about it than the rest."

"I expected that much," Pok said. "That boy couldn't try harder to hide the shame of how he was born. I can only hope not all men who were born as girls feel the way he does."

Roggan plucked off a piece of fish from the spit and put it in his mouth to chew. "He'll soften to her sooner or later, I'm sure. Speaking of softening . . . Nyzai, do you remember how Erku came to warm you over to become your man?"

Nyzai turned her head to face the sun, which had become yellow as gold as it lowered toward the west. A fragment of its glow showed in the tear that drifted from the corner of her eye. "It was not one single thing he did. He was always a handsome one, but we came to like each other over many rains, starting when we had just grown into man and woman. Why do you ask, brother?"

"It's that . . . I think I feel warmth for Oja. But I am not sure what I must do to warm her in turn. I know a lot of men like to hunt to impress their women, but what would impress a woman who can hunt herself?"

"Do you know if she even likes you at all?" Pok asked.

"Well, I remember she showed warmth toward Bukti when we first met her. But, since Bukti has left us, maybe I could give her what he was never able to give her?"

"Like I told you, I don't think you need to do any one thing to impress her," Nyzai said. "If you really want her, you should build it up reed by reed. Earn her trust, show her you care about her, and then she will come to like you the way you like her."

"But what if she still doesn't like me that way?" Roggan asked.

"Then . . . she'll see you as her friend. But if that happens, my brother, I'm afraid you will have to look elsewhere if you want more than friendship."

"You know, speaking of Oja, she might need some company tonight, since she has her own hut now," Pok said. "Why don't you walk over there to join her side, Roggan?"

With a nod, Roggan stood up and picked off another cooked fragment of tilapia from the spit. "That is what I shall do. The poor woman must be hungry anyway."

When Roggan headed over to the hunt-leader's hut, he found he was not the only male of the village who was showing an interest in her. Dako, the village sentry boy, was already standing beside Oja, watching her while she chipped away at a flint spearpoint with a hammerstone in front of the hut. The grin and opportunistic gleam in his eyes were like those of a vulture waiting for a wounded wildebeest to plop dead for the feast.

Oja put down the point and hammerstone to glare up at the youngster with a raised eyebrow. "Shouldn't you be at your post watching for predators?"

"C'mon, one person can't sit there all day," Dako said. "I take turns with two others, and my turn is up for the evening."

"Fair enough, but I don't want you hovering over me like that. I'm too old for you anyway. Find a girl your age to pester."

"Aw, why can't I be with a woman your age instead? It can't be that many rains between us, can it?"

Oja groaned. "Look, young one, I don't want you. Not in the way you want me. So if you don't mind, leave me alone!"

"You should listen to her, Dako," Roggan interjected. "Oja is your new hunt-leader. You wouldn't want to get her mad at you. If I were you, I'd do as she asks. Or run for my life."

"You think she can hurt me?" Dako said.

Roggan stood with hands on his hips and leaned over the boy, back to the sun so that he appeared like a towering shadow before him. "Oh, yes. She can hurt her. And if not her, I will."

Dako scurried away like a frightened meerkat, disappearing from sight within a blink of Roggan's eye.

Oja giggled. "For a man with a bandaged arm, you sure can be scary, Roggan."

"Doesn't take much to scare that one," Roggan said. "How did it go when you met with the hunters today?"

"I think it will take a while to earn their respect. Especially the one called Kore. The way he treated me, you'd think he had been born a boy, too."

"I heard about that. But taking them out on a few hunts should change their feelings toward you. You need to show them you deserve to lead them."

"Which is why I have something planned in honor of the rains' return. I want to hunt hippopotamuses with them. It'll be a feast for the whole village!" Oja spread her arms out wide to show her point.

"It would be if you could bring one down. You do know that hippos, together with rhinos and elephants, are the biggest and most dangerous game out there . . ."

"Of course, I know. That's why I'll have all the hunters behind me. What, did you think I was going to attack one of those hippos all by myself?"

The picture of such a brave but senseless attack flashed through Roggan's mind, making him titter. "Still, you'd want to keep as many men from dying as you can. Don't forget that hippos wade in herds, too."

"Could you have some faith in me, for once? Everyone is always doubting me here. Is it because I'm a woman?"

Roggan did not reply. The answer, much as it would ache to concede it, was obvious, and he did not want to antagonize her more than she would have already experienced that day.

"We will see what you can do when you're ready," he said. "As for me, I've far less reason to doubt you. You did kill the crocodile that mangled my arm, after all. And you did it without any help from Bukti or me. You've earned my respect, that is for sure."

Oja beamed at him. "Then you shouldn't doubt me at all. You know, if that arm is done healing in a few days, you should join us on the hunt." She smiled again. "Will you?"

Roggan's stomach felt soft and fluttery inside. "I will."

CHAPTER NINETEEN
The Pit of Shame

Lu stood at the upper lip of another hole in the earth. This one must have been over twice as vast as the hole he and Tukar had pushed Uru and Namak into, impressive by itself. Gazing into this second, greater hole, he found not only pitch darkness, but a dot of brilliant orange pulsing at its bottom. For all he knew, he was looking into the bowels of the earth, the origin of that flaming liquid rock that spewed from the tops of mountains to the west every so often.

Then he heard voices. Voices which whispered like the wind while bounding between the hole's stony black walls.

"Why did you do it, Lu?"

"How could you?"

"You should not have done that."

The voices did not stop. They grew louder and chanted with greater frequency as they escaped the hole, their message swirling without end within Lu's brain, each syllable chewing at his heart.

"I had to keep Oja away from the band!" he shouted back. "She brings nothing but hurt. She must be gone for good!"

The voices pressed on. They did not acknowledge or respond, instead reciting the same phrases as before. Again and again and again. At the bottom of the giant pit, the orange light glowed bright as a camp bonfire.

"So you think you can push your sister's closest friends into holes?" Lu heard Namak say.

She and Uru were behind him, their bodies conjoined at the sides into one larger being with two heads. Together, they glowered at Lu, their eyes yellow as a leopard's, their snarling mouths revealing sharp fangs instead of human teeth. Even their fingernails and toenails had become hooked talons.

"I did it for the band," Lu said. "You cannot bring Oja back. She only brings trouble!"

"As if you did not bring trouble too," Uru and Namak replied in unison. Their voices melted into serpentine hissing, the pupils in their eyes narrowed into reptilian slits.

They reached out—and found his skin with their talons. They scratched him. Then, with full paws, they pushed him into the hole. They cackled with maniacal glee and whispering voices as he watched their figure shrink along with the sky, while the orange bottom below expanded until he could make out the swirling texture of molten rock.

He stopped falling in midair before he could plunge into the magma. As he floated above the hot liquid rock, it coalesced into giant faces, the faces of everyone in the band. His mother, his father, Uru and Namak . . . everyone. They chanted the same phrases that had tormented him at the top, their eyes white as the sun itself.

"Why did you do it, Lu?"

"How could you?"

"You should not have done that."

They merged together into the face of Oja, his sister, the one he had envied and resented his whole life. Her mouth opened wide, becoming a pit of bottomless blackness, into which Lu plummeted—and kept falling . . .

He awoke gasping for breath.

Lu poked his head out of his shelter. He was still in his shelter. In this world. A world asleep at the darkest moment of night.

The moon hung from its zenith among hundreds of stars, staring down at the world below like a singular, blank white eye. The fire at the center of camp had devolved into a pile of embers with thin streams of smoke wafting upward. From somewhere in the savanna beyond bleated the whooping cries of hyenas on the prowl for prey.

Lu crawled toward the fire, feeling his hands on dirt, a welcoming feeling. He blew a few puffs of air from his mouth. They were just enough to restore the fire to tiny tongues of flame. Not so much that it would awaken the rest of the band, but enough to send an intimidating message to any predators lurking about.

When day returned, he knew one thing: he had to tell the band the truth. This was not something he and Tukar could keep hidden, not if those dreams were to harass his every sleeping moment and remind him of his guilt. Once they made their admission, they had to figure out how to let Uru and Namak return to the high plains if they ever found Oja, assuming they had even survived the fall into the pit.

If he succeeded in killing his sister's closest friends, he would never forgive himself. Nor would the dreams.

The last thing Lu wanted that night was to go back to sleep.

CHAPTER TWENTY
Stones on the Hill

Uru awoke that morning to the squawking of vultures.

The birds had gathered into a mound of black plumage over where the blade-fanged cat's carcass had lain. The racket they made as the squabbling creatures ripped flesh off its bones made her stomach churn, as did the rotting stench the dead body had already started to exude. Nearby paced a jackal that stared at the scene with yellow eyes, awaiting the opportunity to snag a bite after the vultures had stuffed themselves.

If she hadn't lost her spear, Uru would chase away the scavengers, both the vultures and the jackal, and slice off another two slivers of the blade-fang's flesh for herself and Namak. It may have felt weird to eat the flesh of an animal that had tried to eat them, like a reversal of the natural order, but meat was meat, and it hadn't tasted too bad after a little cooking over the fire they had made the previous night. A little tough, but not *bad*.

Her stomach no longer rumbling, Uru crouched in the grass, watching until the carrion-eaters had scattered and left behind little else more than a pile of bones with only slivers of bloody meat. She hacked the slivers off with her knife, gathering as many as she could hold in one hand, and returned to what remained of the fire with a bundle of tinder in her other hand. Once Uru reignited the fire, she cooked the scraps of flesh on a stick like she had the night before.

Namak rose from her own sleep with a deep yawn. "Looks like our morning meal will be lighter today."

"The vultures didn't leave much behind," Uru said. "Had you woken earlier, you could've chased them off with your spear before they ate it all."

Namak picked up her spear and tapped the edge of its obsidian point with her finger. "Where would one find good obsidian around here, anyway? I know this one came from the western mountains, but they are so far away now."

Uru surveyed the southern plains for any mountains or prominent outcroppings that could yield obsidian, the black glassy stone that cut with a sharper edge than any other. There rose from the horizon and beyond distant trees a wide, low hillock on which stood many stout pillars of rock. Some of these pillars stood in pairs that supported a third stone on their tops, forming a frame like a doorway.

Uru pointed at the mound with the upright stones. "Those big hunks of rock must have been set up by people. They could live nearby and have obsidian to trade."

"I don't see any campfire smoke, other than ours," Namak said. "And those rocks look too big for people to move. Maybe it was elephants?"

Uru prodded Namak with her elbow. "You know elephants don't build things like that, silly."

"Then they must have been creatures we've never seen or heard about before, or maybe spirits. Maybe the sun itself set up those stones that way. Who knows?"

"Maybe we should see them up close?"

Namak raised her shoulders with a grunt. "We might as well, while we're out here."

As they crossed the plain, Uru stayed close behind Namak, making sure her friend was always within sight. With only her little knife for protection, Uru would be easy prey for any meat-eaters lurking about. Seldom in her adult life had she felt so vulnerable, like an impala calf that had only started to grow its horns.

She scoured the ground underneath the savanna grass for rocks she could hew into a suitable point for her next spear. Flint and other duller types of rock were never rare, but the same could not be said for the glassy sharp one, the obsidian. She had the option of settling for a flint spearhead, but it would not compare in quality or strength to her old spearhead or Namak's, putting her at a disadvantage.

Just before midday, Uru and Namak walked onto the base of the hill with the giant stones. Up close, their eyes widened to a fuller appreciation for the megaliths' immensity. Each structure had to be at least as long as a giraffe stood tall, and all were stouter than water buffalo. When Uru pushed her hand against one of the upright blocks, it stood more still than a baobab tree. No less than a dozen men must have dragged one up the hill, she reasoned, never mind the grueling final stage—lifting some massive stones on top of others.

They studied the enormous pillars. Carved into each were various images in relief, many speckled with traces of glossy yellow paint. Some resembled the figures of men and women, others the animals of the savanna and rivers, and still others abstract symbols with a significance beyond Uru's ability to guess. One stone featured a pair of concentric circles with lines shooting outward, which reminded her of the sun burning overhead, but she had no way of confirming her interpretation.

At the foot of the megalith was a shallow hole in the earth—and the half-submerged skull of a human being staring up with its empty eye sockets.

"Whoa!" Uru flinched and stepped backward, shivering with chilled perspiration, her yelp loud. She figured she must be staring at some sort of grave that a scavenger like a jackal excavated some time ago. Was this entire assembly of megaliths a place where people buried their dead? The stories claimed that the people of the river villages would bury their dead leaders together in the same place, but Uru had never expected to find one of these areas in her life.

Namak knelt over the hole and pressed her finger into the sediment. "I feel something sharp here. Want to dig it out?"

"No!" Uru answered. "We have to respect the dead. You wouldn't want our graves being dug out and plundered, would you?"

"No, but someone or something else has already defiled the grave. What more damage could we do?"

Namak scratched at the dirt with her knife. With each scraping of sediment, she exposed more of the long, triangular blade of black obsidian, a swirling symbol impressed into the middle of it. Uru's eyes widened as she ran them over the point, as long as her forearm. And twice as long as her old spear's point.

She licked her lips. "That is a big spearhead."

Namak plucked it out of the earth and tossed it to Uru. "Now all you need to do is find a big stick to haft it to. Shouldn't be too hard, should it?"

"And then we try it out next time we need meat. I could kill an elephant with a jab to the heart with this!"

"Don't get too greedy, my friend. We are here in the south to look for Oja, remember?"

"Right, right."

Uru walked back to the dug-up grave and bowed her head to the skull. "Whoever you were in life, thank you so much for the gift."

A chilly breeze grazed the nape of her neck, pickling the little hairs on her skin.

CHAPTER TWENTY-ONE
Confession

"Lu!"

Lu refused to respond. Why was his father calling his name from outside the shelter? He curled up tighter on the ground as if still in a deep sleep, feigning a growly snore. When Aukah rapped a knuckle on the thatching above the shelter's entryway, Lu snored even louder.

"Come on, son, you can't still be asleep at this time of day," Aukah said. "You sure you don't want to go hunting?"

"I didn't sleep well at all last night," Lu replied with a groan. "Find someone else to hunt with you, Father."

"If you say so. It's such a shame that Uru and Namak had to die. They were such good hunters."

The mere mention of his sister's friends sprang Lu to his feet, trembling beneath the weight of his guilt. The vision he had experienced kept replaying in his mind's eye several times, the voices still chanting without end.

Aukah went inside and rested his hand on Lu's shoulder. "Is something wrong, my son?"

After biting his lip, Lu wrapped his arms around his father with eyes starting to flood with tears. "They didn't die. At least, I don't think they did. Tukar and I . . . we pushed them into the underworld."

Aukah froze for a brief moment and then withdrew his hand from his son, taking a step back. His eyelids twitched and then blinked in rapid succession.

"We followed them to this deep pit in the earth and then shoved them into it," Lu continued. "I know not how deep it was, but it seemed bottomless."

"But still, why?" Aukah asked. "Why would you do such a thing to your sister's best friends? Do you not want them to bring her back?"

Lu sighed. "No, I don't. Father, if I may be honest, I've always envied my sister, reckless as she tended to be. Plus, you always seemed to love her more than me."

Aukah slapped his cheek. "What gave you that silly idea? I love both of you the same. Oja was more adventurous and therefore I had to keep my eye on her more often, but do not think that means I value her more! How could you?"

Yuke popped her head through the shelter's entryway. "What is going on between you two?"

Aukah told her what Lu had told him, and she covered her mouth with a loud gasp.

"I thought the band would be safer for it," Lu said. "Oja always brought trouble."

"That doesn't matter," his mother replied. "You do not push people into the underworld! You should tell the whole band about this. Uru's and Namak's families deserve to know the truth!"

She grabbed her son's wrist and dragged him into the center of camp, whistling and yelling for everyone else's attention. It did not take long for the rest of the band to converge into a circle around them, all looking at Lu. The weight of their collective attention felt heavier than an antelope buck's carcass on his shoulders.

"Tell them what you told your father," Yuke ordered in a whisper from the corner of her mouth. "What happened to Uru and Namak the other day?"

Lu swallowed and pushed the trapped air down his throat, resisting the sudden urge to belch. "Tukar and I were the ones who disposed of Uru and Namak," he told the circle, trying hard to keep eye contact with them. "We whacked them into a deep hole in the earth, since we didn't want them to bring Oja back."

Tukar stepped forth from the crowd with a nod. "It's true. Though I did it against my will."

Everyone in the band dropped their jaws open, gasping and cursing in shock.

"You know how to get them back?" Orkit, Uru's mother, asked.

"No, I don't even know where they went," Lu answered. "They could be deep in the bowels of the underworld for all I know."

"Well, unless you figure out how to get our daughters back, I think I speak for all of us when we say we don't want to see your face again!" Neanki, Namak's mother, said as she jabbed a finger toward Lu. "All those in favor of exile?"

"Wait, aren't you going to exile me too?" Tukar asked.

"You just said you did it against your will. I'll have a talk with you later, but Lu is the one who must go. Again, all those who want to see him gone?"

Fists shot up all around Lu and Yuke. One need not count them all to conclude that the vast majority voted in favor of Neanki's proposition.

Lu turned to his mother with teary eyes. "I am so sorry."

"And I would hate to lose you as I did Oja," she said. "But the band has voted you out. All I can say is, farewell."

"And farewell from me to you as well, old friend," Tukar said. "Hope you find another band that will take you in someday."

The circle parted to make an open aisle for Lu to run through. And run he did, racing away until he had the whole camp behind him, hidden from sight by the tall savanna grass. And still he kept on running.

CHAPTER TWENTY-TWO
Planning the Hunt

It was soon after midday when the rain returned once more. It was a gentle shower rather than the intense downpour of the previous day, a soft, soothing pattering on the thatch ceiling of Oja's new home. To best spend the time waiting for the rain to subside, she invited the hunters from the village inside her place, summoning their attention with a few blares of the conch horn she found hanging from a rafter near where her hunting weapons leaned against the wall. This meeting, if nothing else, would give her the opportunity to plan out the big hippopotamus hunt, and maybe get to better know the men who would answer to her as their hunt-leader.

Oja asked her hunter-guests to assemble in a semicircle in the middle of the room, facing her. They were all the same men she had encountered the day her new role had been announced, including Kore, who had not relaxed his characteristic sour frown. The one difference? Roggan was there as well, still with bandages on his arm. So was Dako, the young sentry boy. Despite Roggan's gentle warning to him before, Dako could not take his eyes off Oja any more than most men could take their eyes off a succulent chunk of meat.

Oja overlooked Dako's unwelcome attention toward her, knowing the reason she brought him to the gathering. She cleared her throat. "Alright, brave hunters of the Monitor Village, what do you know about hunting hippopotamuses?"

Dako was first to hold his hand up, shaking it with a childlike excitement. "It's dangerous and could get you killed."

"C'mon, everyone knows that," another hunter said. "I believe she's here to tell us how to make it less dangerous. Or at least hear from those of us who truly know."

"And how does our woman here plan to achieve that?" Kore asked.

Oja bristled inside at Kore's emphatic utterance of the word "woman." "Well, we know hippos spend the day lazing around in the river together," she said, maintaining the even tone of an unaffected leader, irritated though she felt. "Come nightfall, they come onto land to graze."

"So will it be easier for us to attack at night?" Roggan asked.

"Depending on how well they can see at night, I don't know if we could sneak up on them easily. They may look fat, but I know they can run fast on land."

"Wait, if hippos usually gather in groups, would it not be easier—and safer—for us to separate one from the rest somehow?" Kore suggested.

Oja nodded, pleased that Kore had something useful to offer besides mean barbs and glares. "That is just what I am thinking," she said. "We know hippopotamuses are ill-tempered creatures. If one of us were to irritate a single hippo of the herd, perhaps one of the large bulls, we could lure it away into an ambush."

She looked at Dako, as did the grown men in her audience. The boy hunched his shoulders with a nervous pout.

"Dako, would you be willing to be the 'bait' for our hippo then?" Oja asked. "You seem like you'd be very eager to please me."

Dako shook his head. "Not . . . that eager."

Kore gave the youth a grin, wide and mischievous. "Maybe this will motivate you, then. If you carry out your task and survive, the woman will give you a kiss."

Oja snarled with disgust. "No, no, I'm not going to reward him with that, you filthy-minded jackal. Don't you dare pretend to speak for me or know my intentions! But he will earn my respect and maybe make him more of a man." *And far more of a man than you'll ever be, Kore,* she wanted to add, but left the comment on the tip of her tongue.

Roggan snapped his head at Kore with a fierce look in his eyes. "Of course, given how you've been giving our new hunt-leader such a hard time, Kore, maybe you could be the bait instead."

Kore swiped his hand at Roggan, who ducked to avoid a stinging slap. The rest of the men exploded into fits of laughter.

Oja blew through her conch horn again. "Enough! We'll use Dako to lure the hippo into our ambush. Then, we'll surround it and attack with our spears until it tires or bleeds to death. Does that sound like a good plan?"

Kore shrugged. "Sounds as good a plan as you could come up with. Still a bit risky, if you ask me."

"No one asked you!" one of the hunters said with irritation at his attitude. "Give her a chance to lead us on this hunt, would you?"

"I don't think you can hunt hippo without any risk whatsoever," Roggan said. "But it should be worth it. We'll have more than enough meat for the whole village once we bring it down."

"And that is what we should be looking forward to," Oja said. "Trust me, the more we work together on this, the less likely anyone will die or get hurt. Who's with me?"

She held her fist up into the air. After a pause, the men lifted their fists to join her, one by one. Even Kore and Dako did so, to avoid being hopelessly outnumbered.

Oja turned to face Roggan. "How are your wounds faring?"

Roggan peeled off one of his bandages. "Oh, my arm's almost as good as new again. I shouldn't have any problems on the hunt."

"Good. I'll have you scout for hippos nearby tomorrow, if the weather allows, and then we'll get everyone ready for the attack."

CHAPTER TWENTY-THREE
Hippo Hunt

Dako gripped his bow with a clammy hand as he tiptoed through elephant grass that grew taller than himself. The balls of his feet squished into damp, stinky mud even when he tried not to apply too much pressure to them. His whole body dripped with sweat, summoned not only by the day's humid heat, but also by the dread rattling within him.

Why could Oja not have enlisted one of the older, stronger men to be the bait instead? Was this her way of getting back at him for doting on her too much? If so, how could the woman be so ungrateful? Women were supposed to like it whenever a man showed interest in them. Even younger men. What made Oja so different?

If he were to die today, the whole village would blame her for it. They might even cast her back into the bush. Then, at least, he would have a sort of revenge, even if he had to enjoy it from the abode of the deceased within the sun's embrace.

He kicked a heap of mud off the bank and growled in a fit of anger. Then he stopped, wanting to kick himself. If the hippos were nearby, they might have heard that. Did they? Cursing himself for losing control, Dako shrank back into his stealthy posture and resumed his quiet advance down the bank.

Besides, if everything went according to the plan Oja had laid out, she might appreciate the vital role Dako would have played in it. Maybe she would even come to like him the way he had liked her, at least more than she had before. The thought blessed his heart—and his manhood—with a slight touch of warmth.

The grass gave way to a thick screen of papyrus reeds that demarcated the water's edge. Dako lowered himself to a crouch and poked his head through the reeds until he could see the breadth of the river beyond them. He tucked his bow closer to his body, hugging it like it was a protective charm.

A few strides before him, he spotted a score of hippopotamuses half-submerged in the water, resting. Most of the animals appeared to be sleeping or otherwise doing nothing, while a pair of large bulls yawned at each other at the far side of the herd, letting out deep roars and showing the ivory blades that cut up from their lower jaws. Those were not yawns of weariness, but rather the yawns of hippos ready to battle. The contest between these two brutes took a bloodier turn when they started slashing at each other's thick necks, splashing up gallons of water and suppressing all other sound along the river.

Dako had heard that a fully grown hippo was capable of chomping a crocodile in half with one bite. He saw little reason to doubt that claim now.

Eventually the smaller of the jousting bulls retreated and waded away from the others, disappearing into the reeds on the opposite bank of the river. The victor declared its triumph with a thrash of its head and a final roar.

Dako smiled. There he was: the bull he would lure to his hunting party. No other beast in the herd would be so easy to provoke.

Dako took an arrow from his quiver, nocked it to his bow, and focused his aim on the big bull hippo's head. His arms trembled with building fear as he pulled the string back, causing both bow and arrow to waver in his grip. He prayed to the sun that he would not miss, that the whole herd would not charge and trample him if he hit the wrong hippo or spooked them in any way.

He let his fingers slip off the string and arrow. Arcing over the wading herd, the arrow's barbed point buried itself into the rear of the big bull hippo's skull.

The beast let out a throaty bellow as it barreled through the water toward Dako. The young hunter dashed from the bank, forcing his skinny legs to propel him as far away from the charging animal as they could. Grass and reeds slapped him as he ran, slowing him down while the stomping hippo drew nearer. It was not long before Dako could feel the creature's hot breath blasting onto his back.

With a swing of its head, the hippo swatted Dako high into the air. He landed with a hard crash several yards away, the cracking of his spine audible. He could not get up even as the ground beneath him shook under the weight of the monster advancing toward him, determined to finish its attacker off.

Something long and narrow, a throwing spear, whooshed into the attacking creature's plump rear. The beast stopped in midcharge to bellow at whatever hit it from behind. Out of the nearby grass sprinted the other hunters, yelling their battle cry, forming a semi-circle around the hippo and hurling more spears at it, realizing they also needed to protect young Dako, who had done his job—and well.

Even as the assault tortured the beast and drained its blood, the hippo did not back away. It roared at its tormentors as it hurtled itself toward Kore, the nearest hunter, and snatched him up in its jaws. As the tusked animal thrashed him about, Kore hammered its lower jaw with his fists in valiant desperation. Were the beast to bite down harder, his young life would end in a snap.

Another spear plunged into the hippo's eye. Oja's spear. She ran up to the beast with her knife drawn while it roared in anguish, releasing Kore from its gaping mouth. He rolled to the ground. The half-blinded giant was reeling about when Oja wrapped one arm around its neck and stabbed it in the skull, her blade penetrating to the brain. Before she could pull out the weapon, the hippo threw her off with a shake of its head and then lurched onto its side. Its ribs splintered under its weight while blood flowed in rivers from its wounds.

Soon, the bull hippo's breath shallowed into fits and starts, shorter gasps, then silence. It lay there, dead.

After he managed to lift himself onto his feet, Kore helped Oja up. He stared into her eyes with both hands on her shoulders. "You . . . saved me . . ." he said. "You, the woman . . . saved me."

Oja smirked. "And you thought women couldn't hunt as well as men. Besides, I couldn't let you die. I am your hunt-leader. I look out for everyone out here."

Some distance away, Roggan hauled the injured Dako onto his shoulder. "You did good today, Dako."

"But . . . my back hurts . . ." the boy said.

"It will heal. Like my arm. Consider it a hunter's sacrifice. The important thing is that the hippo has been slain and there will be meat for the whole village."

CHAPTER TWENTY-FOUR
Celebration

Even though the moon and stars were obscured by a sky blacker than tar, the village of the Monitor people could not be more awake.

Villagers gathered in a vast circular arena of beaten earth in the eastern wing, taking their seats on reed and hide mats that they had lain along its megalith-lined edges. In the center of the plaza, the choicest hunks of hippopotamus meat roasted on a spit over a bonfire, surrounded by baskets and bowls filled with fish, fruit, tubers, and other tasty foodstuffs the villagers had prepared and contributed. The firelight danced over the spectators' faces to the rhythm of drumbeats, trilling flutes, and singing from an ensemble of musicians who sat at the plaza's eastern edge.

Toward the bonfire strutted the chieftain Nyzai, Oja and her hunters following in a line, carrying their spears the way Nyzai carried her scepter. All the villagers' eyes were fixed on them, especially Oja. The last time so many people had noticed her passing, their attention had oppressed her with embarrassment and a feeling of being unwelcome. Now she welcomed it, holding her head high as she beamed with pride.

The chieftain stopped in front of the fire and tapped the ground with the butt of her staff. The music and chattering of the crowd stopped while the hunters assembled in a ring around the fire, with Oja standing next to Nyzai.

Nyzai held her arms outstretched. "People of the Monitor Village, it is with much gratitude that we all welcome the return of the rains, after so many moons when they did not fall. It shows that, even if our mother the sun takes more time to summon them in certain years than others, in the end, she will always bring them forth."

The question flashed in Oja's mind how the sun, of all things, would have the power to summon the rains every year, but she would not dare interrupt the village chieftain now.

"In honor of the rains' return, we hold this feast, sharing everything we have gathered," Nyzai continued. "Not least of which is the hippopotamus that our hunters have brought down, guided by none other than the newcomer named Oja. Let us all show our new hunt-leader our thanks for her courage and leadership!"

The feasting circle thundered with everyone's applause. Then they chanted Oja's name in an escalating rhythm. "O-ja! O-ja! O-ja!" The sound filled her with an ecstatic pride beyond anything she had felt before. The drummers even pounded their instruments to accentuate the clamor. Oja raised her spear to the sky and yipped a proud cry of victory to the night sky, the other hunters joining in as if to amplify her voice.

"And now, let the feasting commence!" the chieftain concluded with a harder bang of her scepter.

The ring of people held clay platters and assembled into straight lines that converged on the piles of food between them. Each person helped themselves to handfuls from the baskets and bowls before returning to their mats. Oja and the other hunters cut off shreds of meat to distribute among the villagers. Once each of the villagers had obtained their first helpings, it was the hunters' turn to treat themselves before retiring to sit among the others. Nyzai was the last to serve herself food. She then sat with her family.

Oja took her place on a mat next to the chieftain and bit into her share of hippo meat. It was not as fatty as she had expected for such a rotund animal, but savory nonetheless, very much worth the risk of slaying the beast. She would look forward to eating the leftovers over the remaining moon.

A hand tapped her on the shoulder. It was Kore, smiling at her with a sincerity she'd never observed from him. Or imagined possible.

"I never had the courage to admit it before, but my family and I owe you everything for saving my life," he said. "I don't care that you are a woman. You can hunt as well as any man."

Oja felt a warm blush inside her cheeks. "You should have seen my friends Uru and Namak from the high plains," she said. "Also women. Without them, I couldn't have lasted as long as I did. Why, they saved me from a leopard not so long ago."

His eyes sparkled. "Tell me the story."

"Well, the three of us were hunting gazelle, and a leopard took the one gazelle we had injured with a spear's throw. The last dry season was a hard one, and we were starving, so instead of letting the leopard steal our kill, I tried to take it back. Not a good idea. The leopard pounced on me, tearing my skin apart with its claws. Had Uru and Namak not drawn it away from me and scared it off, and gotten wounded themselves, the leopard would have had two kills that day. Maybe more."

Oja looked toward the north, toward her people, her eyes melting to liquid. "Because of my foolishness that day, my friends told me they would never take me hunting with them again," she said, her voice cracking as her eyes filled with tears. "So the morning after the next day, I snuck out of camp to hunt on my own. Like I told you before, I attacked a rhino, and it drove me off a cliff into a river in a canyon, and that river carried me away to . . . your part of the world."

"I see." Kore said it with an empathetic gentleness. "Do you ever miss your people on the high plains?"

"I do. But I don't see how I could ever return back to them. It would be like climbing out of the underworld. And all of you, especially Nyzai, Roggan, and"—her voice caught for a moment—"Bukti . . . have accepted me as one who can live among your people."

Oja felt Roggan's hand on her shoulder. He had left his own mat to take a seat beside her, a gentle smile stretched across his face.

"And you have found another group of people to call your own," Roggan said. "Now, if you don't mind, can you and I have a word together in my family's hut, away from everyone else?"

"Yes." She turned to Kore. "Thank you for what you said to me. You were very brave on the hunt today."

Oja let Roggan lead her away from the feast through the eastern side of the village. With all the people and firelight concentrated in the big plaza, the rest of the settlement was silent and dark, almost a giant version of the abandoned camps her band would occasionally stumble upon on the high plains. The only activity Oja could spot was the odd village cat skulking through the shadows or darting after rats across the street.

They arrived in front of Roggan's family hut beside the base of the chieftain's central mound. It had only been a few days since Oja had slept in there, and that for only one night. Nonetheless, she felt a strange warmth when Roggan led her inside, like she was revisiting a place from her memories. Even in the cover of darkness, she could make out the familiar baskets dangling from the rafters, although they had been emptied of food to be donated to the feast.

Roggan turned to face her, placing his hands on her shoulders. "Oja, there is something I wish to ask of you. You see, never in my life have I seen a woman like you. You are far braver and stronger than most people I know, man or woman. Not only did you save my life from that crocodile when we first met, but you would then save the life of the man who disrespected you—and led us on a hunt to bring home meat for the whole village. As you said you would.

"I do not stretch the truth much when I say that many men would desire you, Oja. Not only are you a good hunter, but I believe you would make a good wife and mother as well. Which is why I ask, what must I do to become your husband? What must I give you so that you would become my wife and mother of my children?"

Oja blinked as she took a step back. "You . . . wish for me to become your wife? Roggan, we haven't known each other for that long. It's too soon. You seem overcome with desire, like a lot of men out there. Give it time."

"So when will it be time, Oja? Until the rains pass? Until the rains afterward pass? Ever?"

"It depends. I can't tell you when I will be ready. But not now."

Roggan's glistening eyes seem to bore into Oja's. He withdrew his hands from Oja with a defeated sigh.

"Then forgive me for all that," he said. "Let us return to the feast. They must be missing us."

Even as they did so, deep in the recesses of Roggan's mind, he had not given up. He would find a way to change Oja's mind, to make her love him sooner. But how? What could a man do that would make a woman swoon for him, or at least show her how worthy he would be as a husband? It was not like Roggan could impress a woman who could hunt for herself with a kill of his own.

Maybe he could give Oja something else, a token of his love, a token showing how much he cared about her. Something more precious than gold, something not everyone could obtain.

As he looked to the stars in the night sky, which twinkled like those rare clear stones called diamonds, Roggan snapped his fingers. He knew exactly what he would give Oja now.

CHAPTER TWENTY-FIVE
Digging for Diamonds

Everyone in the Monitor Village knew of the stream that flowed into the great river from the valley of the ape-people, since each had to travel that upstream path to find the gold nuggets needed to become adult members of the village. It was not the river's only tributary, yet far fewer people knew that another one flowed into the river further east. Roggan expected only he and his father, Pok, knew about that second tributary. It was supposed to be a secret passed down from father to son in their lineage.

After a morning meal of leftover hippo meat and marula fruit, Roggan told his family, "I'm going to replenish our stock of fish." Then he headed to the riverbank where their canoe was moored, though his real intentions were different. But not an outright lie. Depending on how long his adventure took, he might harpoon something to feed himself and have some remaining for the rest of the family. Or he might find game along the river or its tributaries. Nonetheless, Roggan would not tell them what he was pursuing. That he would reserve for Oja once he came back with it.

"Shouldn't you bring someone along?" Pok asked. "You know you aren't the best at fending off danger."

"Don't you worry about me," Roggan replied. "I won't go too far. Just a short trip downriver."

That, too, had only been half-false. At least, he hoped he would not have to travel far to find what he wanted.

He pushed the canoe over the muddy bank into the river, climbed into it, and began paddling down the current. From the bank opposite the village, a herd of hippos were wading into the water after a night of land grazing. Roggan wondered if this was the same herd whose bull his people had killed. He made sure to keep his distance, accelerating his paddling until they were far behind him.

On his right, a crocodile hissed while reclining on a rocky islet that poked up from the surface. Without Oja or the fallen Bukti to protect him, Roggan wanted to attract the flesh-eating reptile's attention even less. Again he paddled faster, keeping his eye on the crocodile to make sure it did not notice him. When it disappeared behind him, he whispered his thanks to the sun for the good luck.

Roggan looked out. He had left sight of his village, with the trees and reeds along the river hiding its easternmost area from view. He continued until arriving at the spot where a narrower stream entered the main river from the north. This had to be the tributary he sought, so he steered his canoe left to enter it.

Morning segued into midday. The tributary shrank in width the further he paddled up its course until it ended at the foot of a low cliff, a waterfall hissing over it. Slathered in sweat from the rising heat and exertion, Roggan stepped out of the canoe, dragged it up the gravelly bank, and treated himself to a cupful of water, spilling it both down his throat and onto his brow. He took out his oar from the canoe and used it to shovel a hole in the sediment.

It was not gold Roggan sought now, but diamonds. He knew they came down this tributary; that was the biggest secret passed from father to son, although every man in the chain typically claimed it to be more legend than fact. Nonetheless, if Roggan could unearth one of those clear, unbreakable stones and present it to Oja, it would impress her even more than gold or any other material the earth could bear.

He enlarged his hole in the tributary's bank, transforming it into a deep crater as the sun drifted westward from his zenith. Still he had not found anything other than lumps of gravel. Roggan walked a few paces closer to the cliff and waterfall and dug there, applying every bit as much effort as he had the previous hole.

Still nothing but rock and dirt.

Maybe he would find better luck further along the stream, even though the cliff prevented him from rowing up its course. He trekked parallel to the cliff until it sank low enough to climb up. Next, he headed to the point where the stream poured over the edge. Beside the top of the waterfall, Roggan began scraping out his third hole.

His arms were ready to explode from strain when he found a morsel of transparent rock embedded in the sediment. Roggan pried it out with his fingers, held it up so the sunlight would beam through it, and laughed with triumphant joy. *A diamond! At last!* He couldn't wait to present it to Oja as his token of love.

Roggan tucked the diamond under the rim of his woven-reed skirt and turned. He stood face to face with a lioness now hurtling out of the tall grass toward him.

Horrified, he yelled and raced across the stream, only for another of the big cats to charge from the opposite bank. He slapped its face with his dirt-encrusted oar and ran upstream until a third lioness lunged at him, forcing him to retreat to the lip of the cliff. The three felines had Roggan trapped between their claws and fangs and the drop behind him.

He swiped and jabbed his oar like it was a spear at the encroaching lions, cursing himself for not having brought his harpoon from the canoe. One of the tawny predators swatted his makeshift weapon with its paw, snapping it in half. Now disarmed, Roggan stepped back and peered over the cliff to the stream below the waterfall. If he could not drive the cats away, he had only one chance of escaping certain death.

And so he jumped.

He splashed into the stream, sinking deep until the coarse gravel of its bed stabbed his skin. Once he floated back up, he breast-stroked to the bank where his canoe lay. He had not yet reached it when the three lionesses leaped off the top of the cliff, landing on the ground below and hurrying to block his way in a semicircular arc. When Roggan tried to bolt past two of the carnivores, the one in the center slashed his flank with its claws, the force of the blow throwing him back-first onto the earth.

A shrill, yipping battle cry cut through the air.

A woman's voice, but not Oja's.

Suddenly, an obsidian-pointed spear soared over the fallen Roggan into the face of the lioness that had clawed him, piercing the top of its skull. As the mortally injured cat fell limp, Roggan sprang up and dashed to his canoe, ignoring the burning pain in his leg, grabbing his harpoon.

Two women charged across the stream at the remaining two lionesses, one with another spear, the other brandishing a flint knife. Roggan gripped his harpoon tight, ran between one of the two preoccupied lionesses, and stabbed deep into its hip. It whirled around to strike back, but he was able to dodge and then prick its breast. Now outnumbered three to two, the lionesses withdrew, mewling in defeat, their stomachs still hungry, and retreated into the tall grass.

Roggan put his hands on his knees and panted. Once he caught his breath, he looked up at the two women who had saved him. They regarded him with equally great curiosity, questions forming in all their minds. The last thing any of them expected was to see another human; encounters with the lionesses, a hippo, or a crocodile would have been more expected. The women wore hide loincloths like Oja had worn when he had first seen her. *They must have come down from the high plains to the distant north*, Roggan thought. *But why?*

"I owe you my thanks," Roggan said. "But who are you, and what are you doing here?"

Namak continued to grip her spear. "I am Namak, and this is my friend Uru," she said. "You wouldn't happen to know a woman named Oja, would you, river man?"

Roggan's eyebrows raised and his mouth opened. *Were these her friends?* "I found her upriver days before the rains came. She has since become one of our village, leading our hunts. Are you looking for her?"

"We are," Uru said. "She is our closest friend, and we and her family miss her. We did not know whether she is alive or in the underworld."

Deciding the young hunter was safe, Uru walked over to the dead lioness and plucked her spear from its carcass. She sheathed her flint knife on her leg. As Roggan inspected the spearpoint, he noticed a distinctive swirling symbol inscribed into it, the mark of a hunt-leader from bygone days.

"Where did you get that?" Roggan asked, pointing at the ancient spear with a quivering hand.

"We dug it out from an old burial place with giant stones a few days' walk to the north," Uru said.

"Then you dug it up from one of our chieftains' graves! That is a crime against our village."

Roggan walked to his canoe and picked up a spare oar he had kept for emergencies. He took a deep breath, looked over to Uru and back to Namak.

"Come with me in this canoe, and I will row you to our village," he said, his tone open, inviting. "I will tell our chieftain what you have done and then she will decide what to do with you. I warn you, though, she can be harsh about these things. Even more so with outsiders such as yourselves."

Namak placed her hands on her hips with a disbelieving scoff. "Why? Surely she'd be thankful that we saved one of her own from those lions, wouldn't she?"

"She might, but we will have to see whether that nudges her judgment on your behalf."

CHAPTER TWENTY-SIX
The Way Down

The sky over the high savanna grayed again. Lu squatted underneath an acacia tree that had begun to sprout leaves on its thorny branches after the rains' return. Without anyone to help him build a shelter, like those he was used to sleeping in, he would have nothing but the strong acacia to cover him when the next shower fell. And the way the storms were building up on the distant horizon, painting the sky a darker shade of gray, the rainfall would come any moment soon.

He gnawed the bones of a gerbil he'd killed with a stone's throw and cooked over his little fire the previous night. Without his friend Tukar or any other hunter in the band to help, Lu had struggled to find and bring down fresh meat. As much as it wounded his pride, he relegated himself to obtaining most of his sustenance from berries, nuts, and tubers dug from the ground. Such was work for mere children and elders. His sister, reckless as she was, would have enjoyed more luck finding meat on her own.

He had only himself to blame for his misery. His band and family had decreed he could no longer live among them because he'd endangered two of their best hunters. Had he not let his resentment and dislike of Oja overcome his judgment, he would not have become an outcast, forced to starve, forced to live in horrifying loneliness. His only hope? To find another band. Or hunters roaming the savanna for their next meals. Even if he enjoyed such luck, they would cast him out the moment he blurted anything about what he had done to Uru and Namak. No man could keep a secret forever. He shook his head. Only himself to blame for that.

Lu's anxiety swirled inside like badly digested chaos.

The frantic beating of hooves on the earth startled him. A stray wildebeest galloped past, pursued by a whooping pack of hyenas. One of the spotted flesh-eaters seized the fleeing ungulate's hind leg with its jaws, dragging its prey to a halt for the other hyenas to tear into and savage. He did not want to be in view when the rest of the clan gathered to devour their kill. Hyenas, like other savanna predators, did not appreciate potential competition for meat hanging around, and those that had not gotten their fill of wildebeest might want to eat him next.

There was only one smart thing to do, and that was to escape the scene.

He ignored the approaching drizzle as he ran from the hyenas and their feast. He ran even after the drizzle built up into a robust shower, pelting him with raindrops and turning the soil to mud.

He slipped, landing with a splat on his back. After he pushed himself back up, he ran some more.

Then his feet touched the edge of the world.

The cliff dropped further down than a giraffe stood tall, a flat grassy terrace of land projecting from its face. The rain and mist shrouded everything beyond this terrace in opaque gray. Lu had a good idea how far south he had traveled since leaving the band, leaving him little reason to doubt he now was in the low country where Uru and Namak thought they would find Oja. Never had he expected to see that part of the world himself!

Lu took shelter under a thick copse of acacia, bushwillow, and marula trees near the cliff's lip. He waited until the rain came to an end and the mist cleared. Underneath the vivid colors of a rainbow that shot between the clouds, he beheld the rolling vastness of the low savanna beyond the cliff and the terrace sticking out from it. For the most part, it resembled the high plains. The one difference: the scattered clusters of trees grew denser until they merged into woodland alongside a wide trail of water, which meandered toward the western horizon.

What if he could find Oja down there? That would be a big accomplishment, a chance to redeem himself. He could achieve what her friends had set out to do before he and Tukar pushed them into the giant pit. That way, his family and the band might forgive him. Even if they would still not let him back into the band, he would at least silence the dreams. Night after night of the same dreams tormented him; guilt weighed heavier on him than being banished from his people.

Now he faced his immediate problem: getting down to the lowlands. His life would end if he tried to jump from the clifftop. How could he climb down to the terrace that jutted halfway down the cliff? Then climb down again from the terrace to the lowlands? He looked more closely, but could see no ramp or walkway connecting the different heights to one another.

Lu looked up to the trees under which he had sat during the rain and pulled out his flint knife. If he could not find a way down, he would make one.

CHAPTER TWENTY-SEVEN
Reunion

While the rain pattered on the thatched roof above her head, Oja scraped on a tusk she had torn out of the hippopotamus's carcass with her flint knife. Whittling at pieces of wood, bone, or teeth always filled her alone time when friends or family were busy with other chores around the people's high plains camp. How she longed to make that a habit again; it filled her with warm memories. She couldn't count how many days she'd spent in this different part of the world.

She sliced off the final sliver of excess tusk, then straightened her hand to examine her completed creation. She looked down at a tiny figurine of a gazelle, like the one she, Uru, and Namak were chasing down when the leopard had claimed and dragged it away. And started this whole mess that her life turned into. In its flank, she incised three circular faces, with swirling lines indicating hair. The faces represented herself along with Uru and Namak—a meaning no one else in the village could ever guess. And she did not plan on displaying it outside her new hut. Instead, she would hang it from the ceiling as a private reminder of the world and way of life she had lost.

It made her eyes water to think of those days spent stalking and chasing wild game across the high savanna beside the two women who mattered more to her than anyone else outside her immediate family. She recalled the evenings they returned with fresh meat to roast over the fire, the nights they told stories to one another or listened to the elders speak of the bygone days. Not to mention her mother and father, and even Lu, despite how much her little brother would fight and argue with her. Not even the passage of time could heal the wounds.

She missed them so much.

Now, she would spend the rest of her life in the same village standing in the same place along the same river, leaving only to hunt. It would take many moons before Oja came to know the hunters of the village as well as she had the people of her band. Most remained strangers to her, even after all these days.

The rainfall's percussive thumping atop the roof faded away, as beams of sunlight returned to fill the hut. Oja fetched a bone needle, drilled a hole into the ivory gazelle's back end, and threaded a string of rawhide through it. She stood to tie the string around one of the rafters supporting the ceiling, and the gazelle caught a luminous streak of daylight on its flanks as it dangled.

Someone rapped on the edge of the entryway. Oja walked up to find Roggan standing outside with two women behind him. They were not women of the village in woven-reed skirts.

She blinked. She looked again.

She gasped. "Uru, Namak! What? What are you doing here? How did you get down the cliffs? How did you find me?" Tears burst from her eyes as she ran toward her friends with open arms and hugged them both.

"We had a little . . . unwanted help in going down," Namak said. "Your family, and the band, misses you back in the high country, Oja. And now we've found you! We want to bring you back home."

Oja's eyelids fluttered in disbelief. "They want me back? I thought they would have taken me for dead!"

"At first we did, and many may still, but I had visions in my sleep of you calling out to me, telling me you were alive," Uru said. She stared at Oja from head to toe, making sure she was really in front of her, alive. "And they did not lie."

Oja turned her head to face the hut, her new home. She had only begun to settle into life in the village, and yet the people she had left behind, the people she thought had left her behind as well, were calling her to her old home.

"You know what, I've had visions of you too," Oja said. "Perhaps my visions and yours were meant to bring us back together."

"Hold on, there is something we must resolve first," Roggan said.

He tapped the obsidian point of Uru's spear. Oja noticed a swirling line incised into it. "Your friends say they dug this spearhead up from the burials of our chieftains," Roggan said, turning to Oja. "That is forbidden for anyone to do, whether in our village or not. We must speak with my sister to choose the right sentence for your friends."

"Sentence?" Oja asked. "What does that mean?"

"You've never heard the word, Oja? It means punishment, or what you do to one who has behaved wrong."

"And what would that 'punishment' be, may I ask?"

Roggan dropped his head. "I can only hope it will not be severe. Especially since, the moment I met these friends of yours out in the bush, they saved me from lions. But I cannot promise that my sister will be merciful. Come, Uru and Namak, let us get it over with."

"I'm going with you," Oja said. "They're the best friends I've ever known. If the chieftain so much as lays a finger on them—"

Roggan sighed. "Then, whatever you plan to do, you will find yourself in trouble too."

"Maybe so, but I still want a say in how she treats my friends."

"Fair enough, but be careful not to cross my sister too much."

Oja growled. "Oh, I'll cross her as much as I have to."

Oja followed close behind as Roggan led her two friends up the central mound to the chieftain's hut. As they advanced up the slope, Uru and Namak gazed in stunned amazement at the elevated view.

Oja could hear Uru's nervous gulp. "They're not going to have us thrown from the top, are they?" Uru asked. "You can see the whole settlement from here!"

"I don't know what the chieftain will do with you," Oja replied. "I haven't been here that long. I've never seen her deal with an issue like this."

"Yet she holds all the power among these people?" Namak asked. "That's got to get to anyone's head. Such women and men cannot be trusted."

Roggan reached the top of the mound. "I wouldn't dare talk about my sister like that if I were you, plains woman."

Once they crested the mound, they found Nyzai seated on her wooden stool before her hut, lizard-skull-topped scepter in hand. She raised her eyebrows and blinked twice when Uru and Namak crossed her line of sight.

"More people from the plains coming down to our village?" Nyzai asked. "These wouldn't be friends of yours, Oja, would they?"

Oja nodded. "Yes, they're my best friends of all. They've come to call me back home."

He yanked the spear out of Uru's hand and held it before his sister, running his finger along the design in its head. "But first, we must address this, which they claim to have dug up from our ancestors' burials."

Nyzai's eyes widened, her fingers tightening around her scepter until the knuckles shone a shade paler. With a shriek, she pointed toward Uru as if thrusting a spear of her own.

"You dare plunder from our sacred burials, plains woman?" the chieftain cried. "Do you even know what you will bring down upon our people?"

"It's only a spearhead," Namak said. "Calm down."

"*Only* a spearhead? Do your people not bury things along with your own dead as well? Even people of the plains such as yourself should know it is blasphemy to steal from the dead!"

"Please understand, chieftain, I was in great need when I did so," Uru said. "Had I known how much it meant to you, I would never have done it."

"What is this thing you call 'blasphemy'?" Namak added. "Is that something you river people came up with?"

Nyzai swiped her hand past Namak's cheek, her fingernails drawing blood like a leopard's claws. "Do not speak against me any longer! You cannot even imagine what your misdeeds will do to us all. Moons of yet more drought, or storms that will flood the world with rainwater, or fires that will burn everything—if not worse! There is only one thing that can prevent all that, one thing our mother the sun will accept as a sacrifice. Or two, in this case."

The chieftain pressed her hand over her chest. "Both your hearts, burnt in our pyre."

"No!" Oja leapt between Nyzai and her friends, spreading her arms out to shield the latter. "You cannot have my friends put to death like that! You can't seriously even believe something as harmless as unknowing theft deserves such murder. I beg of you, spare them and forgive their misdeed!"

"And there is something else you should know, O Chieftain," Namak said. "This very morning, we saved this man of yours, Roggan, from lions not too far from your village. Would you still have us 'sacrificed' like that?"

The anger burning in Nyzai's eyes dimmed a bit, giving way to surprise. "Roggan, is what she says true?"

"Every word of it, sister," Roggan replied.

"Then . . ." Nyzai paused to gaze up at the sun in the sky, holding her arm above her eyes to shield them from its blinding glare. Oja wondered if the chieftain was consulting the revered bright white circle for its advice on the matter.

"To tell you the truth, I wish I could pardon them for their crime, out of gratitude for their courage," Nyzai said. "Still, even if I were to pardon them, the sun may not, for it is the sun their thievery has offended, and it is the sun whose will matters more than mine. Unless you can name something worthy enough to replace your friends' bleeding hearts in the pyre, Oja, I am sorry to say that they must die." Nyzai tapped the ground with her scepter.

What would be worth two human hearts to the sun above? Maybe those of some beast would do it. They had already burnt the hippo's heart as an offering to the sun on the night of the feast, so they would have to hunt something new. Something mightier than a human being, maybe as mighty as the elephants whose bones and tusks made up the chieftain's hut.

Oja snapped her finger. "How about the heart of an elephant? I even think I know of the one I will hunt."

"Oja, an elephant?" Namak said. "You've learned nothing from your past hunting attempts, have you?"

"She did bring down a hippo while she was among us," Nyzai replied.

"And she saved me from that crocodile in the river," Roggan added, patting the arm the reptile had wounded.

"So she has become a better hunter since then," Uru said. "But still, an elephant? She's not planning to go all by herself, is she?"

"I don't have to," Oja answered. "Won't you and Namak come along too? I could even bring all the hunters with me."

"I am afraid your friends will have to stay among us until you offer the elephant's heart," Nyzai said. "And, while we've never offered elephant hearts to the sun before, this would have greater value as a sacrifice if you slay the beast by yourself. I won't let anyone else go with you."

Oja shuddered at the chieftain's command. True, she may have slain a hippopotamus, but an elephant was even bigger and more powerful, especially the specific elephant she had in mind for her task. It would be like hunting the rhino alone on the high plains. Still, Oja would rather not have her friends' hearts cut out to please the sun these people venerated.

"I'll do it," she said. "If I give you the elephant's heart, will you let my friends go?"

"It will be as you request," Nyzai said. "May the sun and all our ancestors give you as much luck as you need."

Uru and Namak shook their heads at Oja. Namak touched her brow with the palm of her hand.

"One thing before I go," Oja said. "Uru and Namak, if I am able to free you, I will come back with you. This I swear before all our ancestors."

"And if you don't come back at all?" Namak said.

"Better to pray to the ancestors that I do. And besides, I've already come close to seeing the face of death more than once. I can stand to risk it again."

Oja walked down the mound to return to her hut and grab the weapons she needed for the most dangerous hunt in her life. She prayed to her ancestors that it would be enough.

CHAPTER TWENTY-EIGHT
The Heart of Old Wounded

Oja received Roggan's permission to use his canoe after collecting everything she would need on the hunt. She brought not only her longest stabbing spear, but also her bow and full quiver, rolls of hide strips to wrap the heart once she obtained it, a hide bag of dried hippo meat, and another bag stuffed with the tiny white crystals called salt. "Salt will keep any flesh from going bad if you spread it over the flesh," Roggan had said.

Oja pushed the canoe into the water, hopped aboard, and started her journey up the river's course.

Day sank beneath the black mantle of night, after which it would rise again, and then sink once more. The second time the sun came back to glow upon the world, Oja rediscovered the pillar with the gold-striped image of the monitor lizard, where she had met Roggan and Bukti for the first time before rescuing the former from the crocodile. The recent rains washed off some of the paint, but what remained of it dazzled with the same brightness as when she had first laid eyes on it.

After another three days of paddling, Oja found the flat table of granite jutting into the river from the south where she had met Urjah, the man whom, along with his family, the village had cast out because of his whiteness. She landed the canoe and climbed onto the promontory, searching for a trace of the fire she had made. All she could find on the rock was a black streak of soot and a few specks of ash. This was still enough to draw a tear from her eye.

Even if she had never gone to the village further downriver, Urjah would have become her new best friend, someone she would have kept company for the rest of her life. She might have never desired the white-skinned man for a mate, but his companionship would have filled the hole of loneliness for both of them. It was not to be . . . all because of that monster, Old Wounded.

Oja armed herself with her bow, quiver, and spear and stole into the woods beyond the riverbank. The trees' regrowth of leaves from the rains cast darker shadows than she remembered, and the tall grasses of the undergrowth shifted from yellow to green. The buzz of insects, chirping of birds, and croaking of frogs suppressed the soft, measured patter of her footsteps over the damp ground.

It was not long before she stumbled upon the disheveled pile of sticks, thatch, and shattered pottery that had once been Urjah's hut. The structure must have collapsed, or perhaps the bull elephant in his wrath had torn it down himself, so great his hatred of humanity. To see Urjah's lonely, humble abode reduced to a wreck made Oja pause to mourn the man she had known for only a day. Not only had he suffered such a brutal fate, but so had everything he and his family had made for themselves in the land of the castaways.

Oja knelt while looking through the woodland canopy to the heavens, tears filling her eyes as they met the sun. "I will avenge you and your parents, Urjah," she whispered. "I will kill Old Wounded for you."

From the woods behind where the hut had once stood sounded a deep, all-too-familiar rumble. Leaves rustled, branches snapped, and a pair of ivory spears gleamed out of the shadows. The ground shook with each of his pounding steps as Old Wounded emerged from cover.

He loomed even larger than she remembered, his hide still studded with the broken spears and arrows that caused his animosity for humankind. Even the spearhead stuck in one of his tusks remained. The elephant spread his broad ears, swaying his head as if to brandish his tusks while scraping over the earth with his foreleg. His menacing rumble, punctuated with harrumphing, was far louder than a lion's roar.

Oja froze like stone. Over the pounding of her heart, she yelled at herself inside her mind to run, to put distance between her and

Old Wounded, and then to come up with a plan to bring him down by herself. But she could not wake her petrified muscles, even as the hulking beast stomped toward her.

Now within one long pace of her, Old Wounded turned his massive head aside and raised his trunk to the sky as a man might draw a club before striking. With a piercing trumpet, he swung it down at Oja. She sprang into motion, jumping back and sprinting down the overgrown path that led from the fallen hut back to the riverbank.

She veered to hide against a young baobab tree, panting as she took out her bow and nocked an arrow to it. The soil convulsed under her feet as she drew the arrow while crouching in wait for the elephant to storm back into view, with his ranting trumpets announcing his coming.

Once his head poked out from behind the tree, she aimed for his eye and released the arrow. It missed, but only by a little, puncturing the creature's hide over its cheekbone. Old Wounded banged the side of his head onto the baobab, uprooting it. After she bolted away from the toppling tree, Oja pinched out another arrow and prepared another shot while ducking behind a boulder.

She let the arrow fly from her fingers. This time, she had hit the incoming monster where she hoped, in his left eye. Old Wounded stopped in midcharge and threw his head back with a shrill, wailing trumpet, half his vision lost. As the wounded giant reeled to his right, Oja unslung her spear and gripped it with both hands while running toward the blind side of his face.

She thrust the spear at Old Wounded's neck, but the elephant batted her off her feet with his trunk, throwing her against a nearby acacia tree. The tree's rough bark clawed Oja's back when she slid to the ground. The animal started another charge, thrashing his trunk, his good eye facing her, his tusks shining and sharp as ever.

She rolled to her side. The massive monster crashed headlong into the acacia, knocking it over as he had the baobab. Oja leapt to her feet, grabbed her spear and stabbed Old Wounded in the jugular artery. The artery of its life. A stream of blood gushed from the wound. She thrust again, but the elephant seized her spear with his trunk, yanked it out of her grasp, and snapped it in half with a hard squeeze. As Oja reached for the obsidian end of the spear, he kicked her in the brow with his front foot.

She slid over the grass several strides behind him.

Bright motes of shock danced in her vision as she rubbed her forehead, feeling a shallow crack in the bone under the skin. The world seemed to tremble in a confused blur all around her, the elephant having transformed into a towering black shadow with glinting red eyes.

Had she lost her mind by thinking she could bring down such a monster without help? This was about to turn out the way her attack on the rhino had back on the high plains. No, it would turn out even worse.

The black shadow grew before her, the land bouncing with its every stomp. Its trumpeting roar drowned out all other sound, even the voices in her mind chiding her for her inevitable failure. It was the loudest voice of all, the voice with the most fury, the voice that condemned her to die for her errors much like her friends would die for theirs.

But she would not listen to it.

Oja scurried on all fours from the elephant's path, got to her feet, and raced past it. She plucked her spear's upper half from the grass and hurried to another acacia with low-hanging branches, Old Wounded thundering on her heels. She jumped, hauled herself onto the lowest branch, and advanced up the tree as the beast rammed himself into its bole. Oja finally reached the uppermost branch.

And then Old Wounded rammed the tree again.

It lurched into a tilt, its far side lowering toward the woodland floor while it splintered at the waist.

She sprang from her perch before the acacia fell, landing on the nape of Old Wounded's neck with what was left of her spear in hand.

The beast reared onto his hind legs, and Oja dug her fingers into his wrinkled hide to keep herself from falling off while beating away his sweeping trunk with her hand. While squeezing her thighs onto his neck to further secure herself onto him, she hammered her spear-turned-dagger into the roof of his skull, sinking the sharp stone point deeper with each stab. She penetrated the soft, spongy tissue underneath the thick bone.

Then the tip of the elephant's trunk coiled around her upper arm as he hurled her off him.

Oja landed among the branches of the fallen acacia while Old Wounded tottered on his legs, his head lolling in circles while leaking the red juice of life. After one last moaning trumpet, the ancient giant fell onto one of his battle-scarred flanks, shaking the earth one last time upon impact. As Oja finally crawled to her feet, the last of his hoarse breaths faded into silence.

Old Wounded, the terror of the savanna below the northern cliffs who had slain Urjah and his family, was on his way to rejoining his own ancestors. Assuming, of course, that beasts had souls like human beings.

Oja had finished what other hunters had started however many rains ago.

She found something sad about how human aggression toward the creature inspired his murderous rage. Who could blame him for that? Still, Old Wounded had taken the life of the lonely man who had been first to show her hospitality in this low country, and she had to avenge that man, not to mention his family.

She murmured a prayer to thank the elephant for providing his heart to her so that she could set her best friends free. Then she took out her butchering knife and went to work at his breast.

CHAPTER TWENTY-NINE
Leaving the Village

Five more times did the sun and moon chase each other across the sky. It was late morning on the sixth day when Oja returned to the village of the Monitor people with the heart of Old Wounded in tow, sprinkled with salt and wrapped in the leather strips. She had yet to land the canoe on the riverbank when she spotted Roggan sitting there, gazing at her.

"Have you been sitting there since I left?" she called.

Even from the canoe, she could hear Roggan laugh. "I took breaks every now and then," he shouted back.

Once Oja paddled to the water's edge, she dragged the canoe onto the bank and moored it. She got out with the wrapped elephant's heart cradled within her arms like a baby, although it was far heavier than any baby she had ever held.

"I cannot believe you got that elephant's heart by yourself," Roggan said. "Though I see from your bandages that it was not easy."

"You could not imagine how I risked my life to get it," Oja replied. "I will never put myself in such danger again. I pray to all my ancestors that your sister accepts it."

Roggan led her back to the summit of the village's central mound. Nyzai was awaiting them on her stool in front of her hut, but this time with the cat Yowh curled up in her lap. When his little green eyes met the elephant's heart in Oja's arms, the feline licked his lips, finding the huge heart appetizing.

The chieftain put him down and rose to meet Oja. "By the will of the sun, you've obtained the heart after all! And so soon as well."

Oja pinched open the heart's wrappings to reveal a sliver of its dark red flesh to Nyzai. Yowh hopped at it with one paw extended overhead, and she had to raise it high beyond the cat's reach until Roggan pulled him away.

"Does that mean you will let my friends go, O Chieftain?" Oja asked.

Nyzai nodded. "We kept them in a big hole in the northern side of the mound on which we stand, where we keep all our prisoners. Give me the heart, and after I put it away, I will go down to free them."

Oja did as the chieftain said, and the latter carried the heart into her hut. After his sister had come back out and strutted down the mound's far side, Roggan dug into his skirt and pulled out the clear, twinkling stone he had dug from the edge of the waterfall before the lions attacked.

"I meant to give you this," Roggan said. "You know what a diamond is, Oja?"

"I've heard of them, but never seen one," Oja said. "What is their meaning?"

"It's a token of . . . love. My love to you, like I told you before."

Oja shook her head with a sigh. "Roggan, again, we have not spent enough time with each other. I don't plan on staying in this village much longer anyway. If you truly feel for me the way you say you do, you would leave the village, too, so you could follow me back to my home on the plains."

Roggan scanned around them, his gaze flying over the whole village, home for his entire life. "I do wish I could go with you, but I have family here, family who will miss me if I leave."

He clenched his hand around the diamond, swung his arm in a circle while facing the river to the village's south, and chucked the strange rock away.

Oja smirked. "I knew you didn't love me *that* much. Like so many men do around women, you mistook your desire for love."

"You might be right," Roggan said. "I was a fool. I even almost got myself killed getting that diamond. Had your friends not saved me from those lions out there, I would have died."

Knowing what the man had just told her, Oja did not think it right not to acknowledge what he had risked to obtain that token. Only the most sincere man would put himself in such danger.

She patted Roggan on his back. "You're not the first man in all time to have endangered yourself in the name of desire. Or love. Still, do not miss me too much. There should be plenty of other women out there in the world for you. This village already has more than enough of them."

Roggan chuckled. "That must be true."

Nyzai came back to the top of the mound, Uru and Namak behind her. As the chieftain retired to her hut, Oja's friends pounced with their tightest embrace, an embrace she was more than happy to return.

"I am so glad you are alive," Oja said. "I am ready to come home with you, even if I don't know how we'll ever get back there."

"We'll find a way back," Uru replied. "We will look as hard as we can for it."

"And to think you were able to kill an elephant for its heart too," Namak said. "I never imagined you, of all people, could do that alone. You should tell us the story tonight after we leave. The whole band will want to hear it!"

The chieftain came out of the hut one more time. "There is one more thing I want you to have before you go, Oja."

Between her fingers, Nyzai dangled the turquoise amulet Oja had given her so she could replace it with the gold nugget on Oja's necklace. Knowing what the gesture meant, Oja silently untied her necklace, replaced the gold with the turquoise, and dropped the nugget into the Chieftain's hands.

"I will keep this nugget of gold in memory of you," Nyzai said. "I must say you have gone against one thing we have always believed, that only men can hunt. Even after you are gone, I will see to it that that tradition is no more, at least for this village. May the sun and all your ancestors watch over you, Oja of the plains."

It was midday when Oja, Uru, and Namak left the village through its northern entrance. They spent the rest of the day trekking through the woods and over the low savanna, never leaving each other's side. All had new spears Oja brought from the hut, her home in the village. If any of the savanna's many meat-eaters and other threatening creatures harassed them, the women of the plains would be prepared.

Day darkened into evening, and they made a fire. They roasted scraps of flesh they had recovered from a giraffe's half-eaten corpse. Even if the meat was not fresh, Oja was thankful that it was more tender and juicy than the dried hippopotamus she had subsisted on during her earlier journey. Being in the presence of her old friends, her best friends, somehow made the meat taste even more savory than it would have had she eaten it alone, or with the people of the village.

"So, Oja, how did you find your way to that village in the beginning, anyway?" Namak asked.

Oja cleared her throat. "Let me begin a long story."

She told them of her confrontation with the rhinoceros that led her into the canyon and down the waterfall. With a tear in her eye, she recalled Urjah the white-skinned man who taught her the bow and arrow, and the elephant, Old Wounded, that killed him as the beast had killed his parents before. She told of the megalith with the gold-striped monitor lizard, of how she had met Bukti and Roggan in their canoe, and how she saved Roggan from the crocodile in the river. She told of how the two men brought her to their village, and how the chieftain Nyzai needed her to obtain a nugget of the shiny yellow rock called gold from the valley of the ape-people so she could become an accepted member of the village.

She told of how she and Bukti entered the valley, of how the ape-people killed Bukti and she escaped, how Nyzai had proclaimed her the new hunt-leader even though the men of the village were less than welcoming of the news. She told how she had led them to slay a hippo for the whole village to feast on, and then how she had slain the same elephant that had killed Urjah in order to obtain its heart and free them.

By the time Oja had finished, she had worn her throat dry and weak. "So my friends, how did you get down here?"

"If only we had gotten into as much trouble as you did," Uru said. "It began when I had visions in my sleep of you calling out to me, asking why we had forsaken you. It was then that I knew you were still out there. Namak and I went south until we found a huge hole in the ground, and something—or someone—knocked us into it.

"Lucky for us, we splashed into a river under the earth that took us to this cave with glowing mushrooms. We found our way out, but this blade-fanged cat, like the ones that prowl in the western mountains, attacked us. We managed to kill it, but it had broken my spear, so I needed a new one."

"Which is why we dug out the spearhead in that old burial ground," Namak added. "We'd never thought it would get us in so much trouble with those river people. Anyway, a few days afterward, we met that man called Roggan after saving him from lions, and he was the one who brought us to the village. You know the rest, Oja."

"I am sorry you had to spend so much time in that hole in the mound afterward, or so the Chieftain told me," Oja said. "What was that like?"

"Dark and dull, for one, and we were of course afraid you would never return. But, thank all our ancestors, it didn't take as long as we feared. And they did provide food and water for us while we waited there, at least."

"The important thing is, though, we are all free and together again," Uru said. "All we need to do is find that way back up the cliffs to the high plains."

Blades of grass shook and rustled from beyond the spread of the firelight. "I can help you with that."

It was Lu who came into view. Lu, of all people, having come down to the lowlands too!

"Lu, what are you doing here?" Oja asked. "You weren't sent after Uru and Namak, were you?"

Lu hung his head low, his hands behind his back. "As it happens, Tukar and I were the ones who . . . whacked Uru and Namak into that hole. I cannot believe they are still alive as well."

Namak growled as she grabbed her spear. "You wish we weren't either! Why, I ought to—"

She lunged at Lu, but Uru pulled her away by her shoulder. Still she snarled behind clenched teeth.

"Why did you do that, Lu?" Uru asked. "You should be thankful we didn't die!"

"I was afraid you would bring back Oja," Lu said. "Forgive me, my sister, but I was always jealous of you, and I always felt you could put people in danger. It was wrong of me, and I am sorry!"

The boy crumpled to his feet, his cheeks glistening wet from the firelight. Even if he had come so close to getting her friends killed, Oja felt pity for her brother.

"Did the band ever find out?" she asked.

"I told them myself, and they cast me out," Lu responded. "After a few days out by myself, I found a way down from the high plains to the lowlands. Or rather, I made one. I cut down some trees, carved steps into them, and placed them from the top of the cliffs to the bottom. I will show you if you follow me."

"I don't trust him," Namak said. "I never liked him, and I like him even less after what he did to Uru and me."

"I understand, but if he has made a path back home, I think we should let him show us," Oja said. "It would save us so much time searching."

"You are right," Uru said. "I would be happy for any path home, no matter who guides me there."

Namak grumbled. "I suppose I can't argue you two out of it. If the boy keeps his word, then I will be happy, even if I will never trust him afterward."

"No need for that," Lu said. "After I lead you to the way out, I will live on my own for the rest of my life, no longer bothering anyone else. It's what I deserve. You have my word."

CHAPTER THIRTY
Home

After a few more days of walking, Lu and the women reached the path he had made back to the high plains. Like he had described, he had laid logs along the height of a cliff at an angle, and carved a series of steps into them to allow easy passage upward. Having thus delivered his sister and his friends, Lu waved and bade them farewell before disappearing back into the tall grass of the low savanna, declaring that he and they would never see each other again.

Before her adventure down to the lowlands, Oja would have been glad to never see Lu again. Yet, now that the time for him to leave her life forever had come at last, she could not hold back a tear for him. If nothing else, the boy had made up for so much of the grief he had caused them, even if, as he knew himself, he could not be trusted among the people anymore.

The women hiked up the steps on the log to the top of the cliff. To their left lay another log with steps along another cliff, which they also ascended. Once they had come to the top of the second cliff, there stretched before them the high savanna their band, and the other people of the plains, called home.

Oja looked over her shoulder at the lowlands below and behind her, the distant river sparkling in the sunlight as it meandered eastward through them, fringed by a woodland of trees that now seemed puny. If she squinted while tracing her vision along its length, she could make out clusters of yellow cone-roofed objects, which she recognized as the huts of more villages, as well as scattered megaliths and circles of megaliths their people had erected.

It was a world in which she had spent well over a moon's cycle, a world that had almost become her home. But in the end, it was not her world. Nor could its people ever be her own, for she was a woman of the plains, as were her best friends and her family.

Two more days of traveling northward followed before Oja, Uru, and Namak came upon a gathering of domes built of grass and branches. These were not the huts of the lowland people, but the temporary shelters of her own.

Everyone poured out to greet the three missing women, one presumed dead. Foremost among them were Aukah and Yuke. Together they wrapped their arms around their daughter, and she around them. Never in her life had her eyes leaked so much, nor had any embrace she accepted warmed her so deeply on the skin and inside.

"We never thought you would return, my child," Yuke said. "This is a blessing for all of us."

"I am so thankful to be back too," Oja said. "Has the hunting been good lately?"

"I am afraid not as well as it could have been, considering the rains' return," Aukah said. "I am sure that, now that you and your friends have come back, we will have more meat than in the days before."

"And we will look as soon as we can," Namak said after giving her sister, Iyi, and her grandfather, Kulro, an embrace each. "Oja, how does a hunt with me and Uru tomorrow sound?"

Namak gave Oja a wink, and Oja grinned back with a nod.

"I will be more than honored," Oja said.

HISTORICAL AFTERWORD

The novel you have just read takes place in eastern Africa around 100,000 years ago, during the Pleistocene epoch. All the characters represent early *Homo sapiens*, the ancestors of all modern human beings. At least 30,000 years after this time, a subset of these people will disperse across the continent and beyond, eventually populating the rest of the planet. There were multiple waves of hominins that migrated out of Africa earlier, such as the forerunners of the Neanderthals of Europe and the Denisovans of Asia, but the human lineage that stayed the longest in the mother continent before spreading elsewhere is the one we all descend from.

For the most part, the ecosystems of Pleistocene Africa would have looked less alien to modern people than other regions of the world during this time, as the continent would lose a much smaller proportion of its megafauna at the end of the Pleistocene (little more five percent) than would Eurasia (twenty-two percent), Australasia (sixty-seven percent), or the Americas (fifty-four percent).[1] It is possible that, since the wildlife of Africa evolved alongside humans, they were better adapted to coexisting with us than those in other continents. Nonetheless, there are some creatures represented in the novel that are no longer found in Africa today.

The first would be the ape-people, based on the hominin species *Homo naledi*, remains of which have been found in South Africa

---

1 Putshkov, P. V. (1997). "Were the Mammoths killed by the warming? (Testing of the climatic versions of the Wurm extinctions)." *Vestnik Zoologii*. Supplement No.4.

and date between 335,000 and 236,000 years ago. They are remarkable for preserving traits such as proportionately small braincases and adaptations to climbing trees that are more typical of hominin species from a few million years earlier such as *Australopithecus afarensis* and *Homo habilis*. However, they did also have higher, thinner skulls than these previous species, indicating that their lineage had nonetheless undergone some evolution of its own since it diverged from the one leading to ours.

Another extinct species featured in the novel is the "blade-fang" that Uru and Namak encounter in the caves. This is based on various saber-toothed cats like *Megantereon*, *Dinofelis*, and *Homotherium*, which hunted in Africa during the Pleistocene and the preceding Pliocene and Miocene epochs. All these cats would have been smaller and with shorter canines than the famous American *Smilodon* which has become the archetypal "saber-toothed tiger," but they still would have been formidable predators.

As for the human cultures represented in the novel, they are my invention, but both draw on two types of hunter-gatherer cultures that anthropologists have recorded. The people of the plains, Oja's people of origin, have an egalitarian and nomadic culture similar to that of the Hadza of Tanzania and the San of southernmost Africa. These peoples live in dispersed, wandering bands with a flexible membership and a lack of formal hierarchy or governance by a chieftain or other ruling figure.

On the other hand, the people of the river villages, such as the one the chieftain Nyzai commands, are based on sedentary hunter-gatherers like the Tlingit and other Native Americans of the Pacific Northwest, or the Natufians of prehistoric western Asia. These have settled down in permanent villages, often alongside rivers that provide a regular supply of food and water throughout the year, and they sometimes have rulers such as chieftains leading them. Some of these cultures might even erect monumental structures like the massive stone pillars at the site of Gobekli Tepe in Turkey, which date between ten and twelve thousand years ago.

It is likely that, prior to the development of agriculture, early humans would have developed both these types of society, and maybe even more than those two. It would have depended on which environments they settled in, with permanent settlements being more likely in areas where a yearlong supply of food was concentrated in a limited area. In areas where food was more evenly distributed across the land or tended to move with the seasons (as in the case of migrating herds), nomadic foraging would have made more sense as a lifestyle. All in all, human societies during the Pleistocene must have been at least as variable as the environments they would colonize in that time.

We can only imagine what some of those societies must have been like.

CHARACTER ARTWORK

For full-color artwork and more behind-the-scenes info about *Women of the Plains*, visit brandonpilchersart.com/my-books.

Oja

Uru

Namak

Nyzai

Ape-People

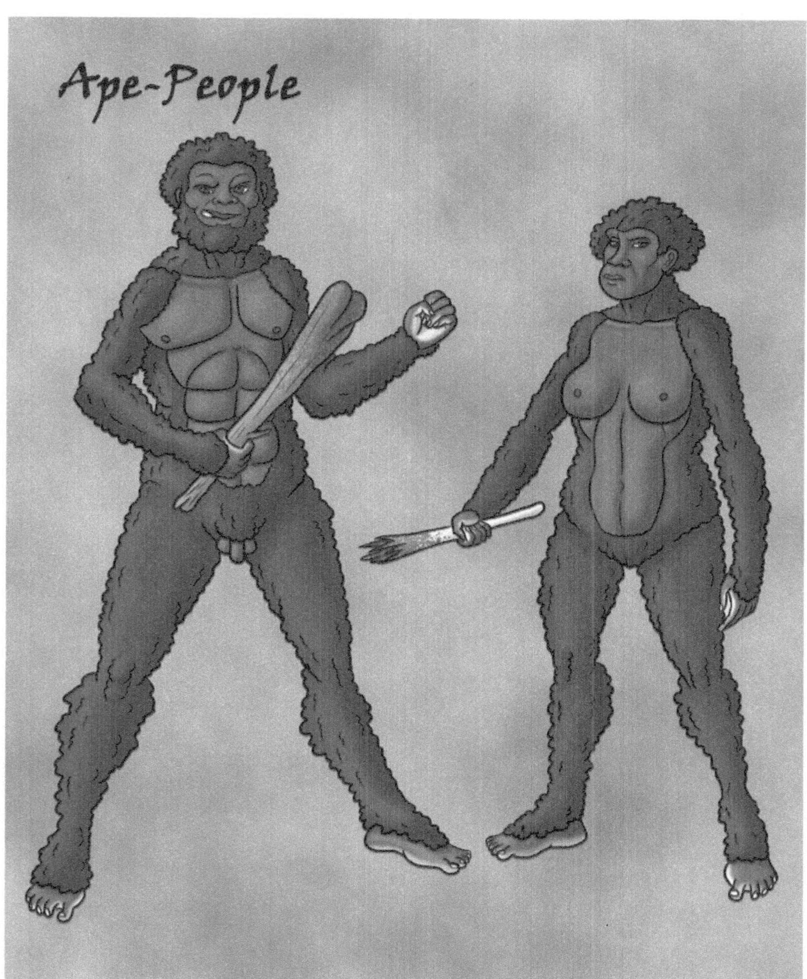

Blade-fang

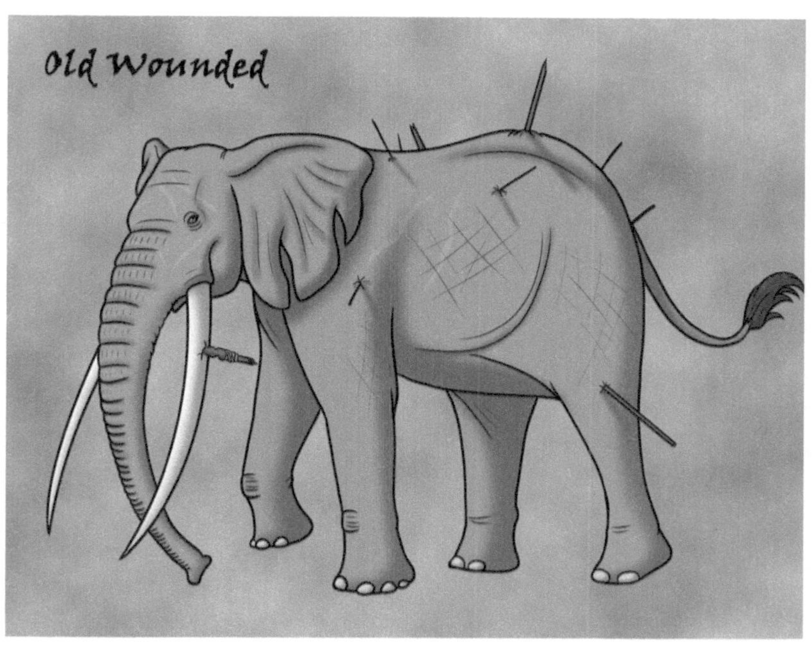
Old Wounded

Other Books by Brandon S. Pilcher

Priestess of the Lost Colony

**A headstrong Egyptian priestess, her brother,
their sacked colony—and a rescue mission.**

When Itaweret's beloved Per-Pehu falls to the tyrannical Scylax, she and her brother Bek lead a mission to save her captured people and depose Scylax. Along the way, they run into all kinds of perils, friends, and foes—and beasts sent by an angry goddess. Set in ancient Greece 3,500 years ago, this is a tale blending magical realism with history, high adventure with discovery . . . and Itaweret's determination to save her people while learning her heart's desires and realizing her deeper purpose.

Carthage Atlantica: An Alternate History

It is 200 BC, and the North African civilization of Carthage is recovering from a brutal war against the Roman Republic. Searching for new lands to colonize so they can rebuild their wealth, the Carthaginians send a fleet across the Atlantic Ocean that lands on the shore of North America, which they call "Atlantis". As they struggle to adapt to this new world, the Carthaginian settlers find themselves drawn into a conflict between Native American nations, a conflict the colonists' own leadership is willing to aggravate in the name of their personal ambitions. Can the colony of Carthage Atlantica survive in this account of alternate history?

The Slave Prince of Zimbabwe

Hailing from the land known as Ruthenia in eastern Europe, Drazhan Khazanov has found himself forced into bondage and brought all the way to the Sultanate of Kilwa on the southeastern coast of Africa. His master the Sultan has offered him a chance at manumission if he can abduct the fierce and beautiful Mambokadzi of Zimbabwe. But when she foils Drazhan's attempts to capture her and offers him an alternate path to the freedom he craves, they find themselves confronting the wrath of not only his former master but also the mightiest empire in the medieval world.

Dinosaurs & Dames: A Selection of Short Stories

By and large, the short stories in this self-published collection are action-packed speculative-fiction tales featuring dinosaurs and other savage beasts, fierce female warriors and huntresses, and African cultural influences. Among our protagonists are a veteran Egyptian warrior who must defend her beliefs and family from the Pharaoh Akhenaten's persecution, a Tyrannosaurus rex hunting for food, a nervous huntress taking on a herd of stampeding Stegosaurus, and a professional photographer and his native guide searching for the perfect shot … and many more!

Beasts & Beauties:
A Second Selection of Short Stories

Brandon S. Pilcher, the author of the stories in *Dinosaurs & Dames*, returns with a selection of eight more action-packed tales of strong heroines of color, fearsome adversaries, and savage beasts. Examples of these tales include a rebellious ancient Egyptian warrior and her little niece who find themselves trapped in a dangerous royal menagerie, a jungle huntress who must rescue her sister from sacrifice to a long-lost god, a trained dinosaur wrangler who must track down an escaped Brontosaurus, and princess who must settle an international dispute through a ball game ... that may mean life or death. And many more!

If you love dinosaurs and other fierce beasts, ancient history, and strong and fierce heroines of color, these are the stories for you!

The Sultan of Finback Isle

Abdullah and Monique Kalua, a daring husband-and-wife team of FBI agents, are on a mission to investigate the Los Angeles Police Department's recent acceleration of corruption and brutality under the leadership of Moroccan-born Ibrahim Fawal. Their pursuit leads them to Fawal's secret winter getaway on Finback Isle, a lost world in the Pacific Ocean where creatures of the Permian Period still roam. Not only must the Kaluas brave treacherous jungle littered with Polynesian ruins and teeming with beasts older than the dinosaurs, but they must also contend with the armed officers of one of the most vicious men ever to head the LAPD ... the Sultan of Finback Isle!